CUPCAKES, CORPSES AND CHAOS

LILA HARROW: A POINT MUSE COZY PARANORMAL MYSTERY BOOK ONE

KELLY ETHAN

 Created with Vellum

CUPCAKES, CORPSES AND CHAOS

Cupcakes, corpses and an underworld jailbreak.
Let the mayhem begin.

Lila Harrow, baker witch extraordinaire stays away from Harrow-caused mayhem in the town of Point Muse, Maine.

All her witchy gifts are poured into her baked goods and her bakery 'Heart's Delight.' But now her cupcake-loving customers are turning up dead and minus a soul...

And Lila Harrow is the number one suspect.

Between a soul hunting Grim Reaper, bakery sabotage and a duo of demon prison escapees out for Lila's blood, a baker witch can't even ice a cupcake. Lila has no choice but to investigate the murders and save her business.

A piece of cake for a witchy baker.

If you like snarky dialogue, murder and mayhem then you'll love the first installment in Kelly Ethan's Point Muse Cozy Paranormal Mystery spin off series – Lila Harrow: A Point Muse Cozy Paranormal Mystery!

<u>Unlock the mayhem of Cupcakes, Corpses and Chaos!</u>

ONE

"Hecate's toenails, I'm blind." Lila Harrow, bakery witch extraordinaire, slapped a hand over her eyes as her father adjusted his bathrobe.

"Don't be such a drama witch." Amelia Harrow, Lila's animal empath and Vet mother, scowled at her daughter. "You're an adult. Seeing your parents in bathrobes shouldn't be scarring."

"It is when they've been separated for years, and bathrobe gaps are involved." Lila narrowed her amber-colored Harrow eyes at her mother. "What gives? Why so friendly?"

Lila's mother sniffed. "We've always been *friendly*, as you call it. It's not your father's fault his boss is unreasonable."

"Now, dearest." Lila's father patted his wife's

hand. "Guarding Tartarus and Hades is an important job. We have talked about this."

Lila rolled her eyes. In her opinion, Hades, God of the underworld, was a needy, clinging, whiny baby. The God couldn't get along without her father, Darius Shade. As a consequence, she'd grown up with a part-time dad. Considering the rest of the family's luck with absent males, her mother was ahead of the Harrow curve. "Hades needs to man up and get a life."

"Lila Marie Harrow," Amelia scolded her daughter. "Never insult a God. You know how they hold grudges."

"I was four and a Harrow. You should never have taken me to Dad's work party."

"It was a daddy-daughter day at work. I expected you to behave. That's all you had to do." Amelia banged a plate piled high with bacon and eggs in front of her husband.

"Now, sweet pea."

Lila ignored her father. "That woman refused to let me have a second cupcake. Told me I'd get fat. I decided she should eat one herself." Lila snatched a serving of bacon off her father's plate and flashed her dad a wicked smile as he choked on a mouthful of food.

"You smashed it into her face and through her hair. She developed a rash and had to see a healer for weeks afterwards."

"I was four. How did I know she had a sugar allergy?" *Persephone, what a sugar hater.* Lila rolled her eyes at her snickering father.

Amelia whacked her husband over his head. "Don't you enable her, Darius Shade." She turned to her daughter. "I'm sure your cousin, Xandie, the mature and responsible Librarian, would never have coated a Goddess in a cupcake."

"She was probably eating her snot and running away from a killer Knight at the same age." Xandie's mother, Miranda, had been chased off a cliff by a knight obsessed with pure-blood humans. To them, supernatural creatures were scum to be disposed of. Thankfully, Miranda had turned up alive twenty years later.

"That's it!" Lila's mother's skinny body vibrated with outrage. She swung around and pointed a finger at her bathrobe-clad husband. "She's your child, deal with her." Every silver-streaked brown strand of hair fanned out as Amelia twirled and stomped out of the room, muttering curses.

"You shouldn't push her like that, she might smother you in your sleep one night."

"First, I don't live at home anymore, so she'd have to break in. Second, she isn't Elspeth."

"Your mother means well." Shade's eyes twitched as he kept his face blank for a few moments before they both burst out laughing.

Lila wiped the tears from her eyes. "Xandie and I are completely different people. She's bookish and responsible with the occasional sarcastic snipe. I'm plain snarky, all the time. Drama is my middle name."

"Actually, it's Marie. But I get your point." Her father coughed before ploughing on, "She loves you, Sugar. She's worried. Xandie has her Library to protect her, you don't."

Last year her cousin, Xandie, had arrived in town and solved her great-aunt's murder. Then she became the Librarian to the supernatural Great Library of Alexandria. Lila had grown close to her cousin and loved her dearly. But she was over her family comparing them. Lila knew Xandie had her own issues with a disappeared, now reappeared, mother, a sentient library, a smart-mouthed cat guardian, and a protective bear shifter boyfriend. But it still annoyed Lila to no end.

"All I'm saying is give your mother a break. She had to be a single parent while you were growing up." He looked down at his plate, his silver-streaked dark hair curling around the nape of his neck. "My job kept me away, but I've always watched out for you. You're my little princess and I've never stopped loving either one of you."

"I know, Dad." Lila patted his hand and stole another crunchy piece of bacon. She used it to point at her father's soft pink bathrobe. "How long has this been going on?"

Her father smiled. "It never stopped. Once we realized how my absence, and then reappearance, constantly affected your behavior, we made sure our visits happened when you were out of the house."

"Aha." Lila crunched bacon and mumbled through a mouthful, "Mom used to act way too happy when I came home from school. No single parent carries on like that. It isn't normal."

"You seemed to settle down and we just continued with the same routine." He shrugged. "Now it's a habit. Your mom gets her alone time and it's even better when we get together."

Lila shuddered. "Don't mention getting together and you guys in the same breath. It'll traumatize me. For life."

"Always my drama Llama Lila."

"Please, I am not four anymore. Can we forget

that nickname and get down to why you let me spring you two in your bathrobes?"

"I explained…"

Lila cut across her dad's words with the slice of her now bacon-empty hand. "Years of keeping your nookie time a secret and I just happened to spring you today? Not to mention mom gave up the opportunity to engage in a good fight? Get real, Dad. What's up?"

Darius shoved his half empty plate to the side. "I never could hide much from you."

"Except for secret nookie time."

"Lila. This is serious."

"Fine. Zip." Lila ran a hand across her closed mouth in a zipping motion.

"Hades sent me to warn you and the Harrows. We had an escape from Tartarus, the underworld jail."

Breaking her promise not to interrupt, Lila burst out with a question. "Why would Hades need to warn us? And who busted out?"

"Two Keres Daimons. Death Daimons. They were a trio, but one of the sisters turned and gave evidence against the others. Hades sent her into witness protection and the other two got a one-way trip to Tartarus."

"But why warn us? Why would they head to Point Muse after a jailbreak? They could go anywhere."

Her father sighed. "That's my fault. I arrested them and they didn't go happily. They cursed me and my line... And that means you, sweetie. I'm sorry."

"You can't control the actions of others, Dad. You do the crime, you do the time, I say. Besides, since Xandie arrived, Point Muse is the murder capital of the supernatural world. Not surprising the escapees would head here anyway." To be fair, Xandie hadn't caused any of the murders and *had* solved them all, but it still wasn't a statistic the town wanted to advertise.

"And Harrows are in the thick of it."

"Not all Harrows...well, not all the time. Just Xandie. I'm the Baker, remember?" Lila waggled her fingers. "No hexing for me, just good old-fashioned sugar overdosing and good vibrations. The Harrow witchy gifts have nothing to do with me."

"That's my point. That's why Hades and I decided to give you some protection." Lila's father cleared his throat. "Amelia, sweetheart? Could you come here?"

If this was a parent-organized blind date, she was out of here. Underworld prison break or not.

Lila's mother staggered into the kitchen with a large armful of black wriggling puppy dog.

"No way." Lila shook her head. "Nope. I am not an animal person, you know that."

Amelia handed the dog over to her husband then crossed her arms, scowling. "You don't have a choice. I'm an animal empath and Vet. You've always been surrounded by animals. Why so resistant to an animal companion now?"

"That's exactly why. There was never any peace in this house. We always had animals underfoot. You were nicer to them than me."

Amelia gasped. "Lila Harrow, what a horrible thing to say. Elspeth would be proud of you. And that's not a compliment." Her mother glared. "Hades wants you to have him and you don't say no to a God, or your father's boss."

"Lila. Listen to me, sweetheart." He calmly stroked the puppy's massive head. "This boy is one of Cerberus' latest litter. He's the runt. The only one that didn't inherit her three heads. The poor boy's father is a hellhound and this one has inherited his dad's genes instead of his mother's. Hades wants him away from his bullying litter mates and he can also help protect you."

That small horse was a puppy and related to a hellhound and Cerberus, the three-headed dog guarding Hell? House training wouldn't be pretty. Giving in, Lila agreed. "Fine, but Hades supplies all the equipment and pays for the dog's vaccinations."

Beaming, her father handed over the dog. "Done and done. His name is Gnasher."

Lila groaned under the weight of the dog. "Gnasher? Hades seriously needs to get a life. I'll call him Nash." She stared into the dog's slightly tinged red eyes. "Nash? That suits you?"

The dog cocked his head and considered Lila for a moment before settling down and half hanging off her lap. The red tinge in his eyes disappeared completely.

Amelia nodded in satisfaction. "I always knew you were a dog person." Reaching into a cupboard, she drew out a box. "This is everything you'll need to start with. Two bowls, one for water, one for red meat. A blanket and padded cushion bed, a few lifelike chew toys, and he's already wearing a collar." She pointed to the pewter tag hanging off a silver-studded black collar.

"Overcompensating or what?" Lila read the tag

out loud. "Property of Lila Harrow, witch. Touch him and die. *Catchy.*"

"Here's the dog manual for hellhounds." Amelia dumped a thick, dusty tome on the kitchen table. "Nash is special. Since he's a mixture of Cerberus and hellhound, we aren't sure what traits he'll inherit. All his brothers and sisters developed early, but this one is a late bloomer." Amelia tickled the snoozing hound under his throat. "But he's intelligent, so don't worry about toilet training."

Thank the gods. Lila groaned as she handed a snoozing Nash off to her mother again. "I'll let you and Hades get away with smothering me one last time. But don't think this is the last time we talk about booty calls and bathrobes. There *will* be a reckoning." Lila grabbed the box of doggy goodies and stomped out, only to return a few seconds later. She cleared her throat and looked over her mother's shoulder, refusing to meet her gaze. "I forgot the dog."

Lila had the feeling that wouldn't be the last time she said those words.

TWO

"Should have named you sugar." Lila turned a corner and spared a quick glance at her hyped-up hound. Nash sat in the front seat of her bakery van, his head on swivel as she drove through town. Once she got back to the bakery after visiting her parents, she'd given Nash a tour. He'd rushed around like a toddler high on sugar. Thankfully, Elspeth owned the building and Lila stayed and worked rent-free with currently no tenants other than herself to complain about. She lived above the bakery, in one of two large apartments. The other tenant left a while ago and as far as she knew, Elspeth hadn't found anyone to take over the apartment yet.

Nash panted and lowered his head, *thankfully only one,* onto her lap. "Maybe you're growing on me, because you *are* kind of cute. At least you don't look up women's skirts like Elspeth's pug or cough up fur balls in my shoes like Xandie's cat, Theo, does." Two decrepit old hags crossed the road in front of Lila's van, and she slammed on the brakes. The van slid to a grinding halt in the middle of the road. One of the women raised a clawed hand in a typical hand signal. Then the other woman dragged her friend to the side of the road before they disappeared around the corner. "Point Muse. Always a crazy or two." Lila pulled around in front of Geri Kerr's messy shop. The old woman had become addicted to Lila's Blue Moon Serenity cupcakes and her Vanilla Viagra ones as well. Geri, crotchety old antiques dealer, needed all the serenity or vanilla Viagra that Lila's witchy baked goods could give her.

Lifting his head as Lila hopped out, Nash whined softly. "Sorry, Nash. Geri is mean and grumpy, without the benefit of being related to me. You stay here. I won't be long." Lila grabbed a container of cupcakes and waved to Nash. She paused at the front of the curio shop and frowned. The store seemed deserted, shades down and no sign out on the sidewalk. That wasn't normal. A stickler for a nine to five routine, Geri wouldn't normally close the shop for another hour. Lila rested the cupcakes on her hip and knocked on the door. "Geri? You there? I have a cupcake delivery." She turned the old-fashioned metal knob and the door swung open with the obligatory, horror movie squeak.

Nash sat up and barked like crazy, pawing at the car window.

"Calm down, hound. I'll be back in a moment." Lila stepped into the store and closed the door behind her. "Geri? It's Lila from the bakery." All the lights were off and the sun from outside only reached so far into the crowded store. "Hecate's sharp toenails," Lila cursed as she knocked her shin on the sharp edge of an upended box. Geri's shop was a curio store, packed full of a mix of kitsch and valuable items. Lila called it hoarding. Geri hated to throw anything out. And watch out anyone who complained about the mess. The sour old woman would let loose a spray of vitriol. She was also one of Lila's best cupcake customers.

Same day, regular as clockwork, Geri would order a straight dozen cupcakes. Each week a different flavor. Today's offering was a favorite, Blue Moon Serenity. Most of the Harrow women had superior witch skills. All Lila had was an obsessive love of sugar and baking. And any witchy gifts she did have went straight into the baked goods for her bakery, *Heart's Delight*. The yummy cupcakes, cakes, bars, or anything with sugar, had a reputation in Point Muse. Feeling low and in need of a lift? Head to Lila's. Need a special boost of self-confidence, go to Lila's. Her food made people feel good and helped them focus on what they needed in their life, what was important. She poured any magic she'd inherited from the Harrow bloodline into her baked goods. That's why she had to be careful when baking. Moody, down, or upset, her feelings transferred into her baking. No one wanted a customer crying over a plate of cupcakes. Her bakery was the soul of Point Muse and if Lila could give a little serenity to crotchety Geri Kerr, all the better. *Speaking of Geri...*

Keeping a tight grip on the box of cupcakes, Lila stepped gingerly further into the shop. But then she went flying as her foot slid on something wet. She hit the floor but twisted at the last minute and landed on her hip, saving her cupcakes. "Goddess, that hurt. At least the cupcakes are safe." Lila put the box on the ground and rolled onto all fours. Something thick and sticky coated her hand. "Yuck." She cringed and scooted back until she hit something soft and squishy. Something that moaned as she touched it. Something that sounded an awful lot like someone groaning. "Geri? Are you okay?" Lila turned and stared at the shadowed area where she'd heard the sound. She could make out the shape of a prone Geri, but little else.

"It's okay, I'll get some help."

Geri's hand shot out and latched onto Lila's wrist. "Too late," she mumbled, and her hand drifted away from Lila's wrist.

What had she meant, too late? Lila straightened as she heard the tinkle of shattering glass and peered outside in time to see Nash crash through her van's window and launch himself against the shop door.

Distracted by her hellhound, Lila never heard someone approach her from behind. But she did feel the crushing pain that explode in the back of her skull. The shop tunnel-visioned and black shadows obscured her sight. She fell against Geri's collapsed body.

Her last thought? The bill she'd present to Hades for her van's smashed window...

***

"And that's why dogs are crotch sniffers and felines are superior." Theo twitched his whiskers as Xandie removed him from Nash's mouth.

"Hush you. He only wanted to play with you."

"How do you know, my oh-so-not-knowledgeable Librarian?"

"There's no blood, now shush. Lila has a headache."

Xandie finished making a sweetened tea and placed it in front of her cousin. "Have this, sugar's good for shock."

"So are frozen vegetables." Holly hefted a frozen bag of peas and placed it gently against Lila's bump-swollen skull.

Lila adjusted the vegetables. "Make sure you give the invoice for my broken window to Mom. She can pass it to Hades."

"You should be thanking him, not billing him." Amelia popped into the kitchen. "What did we tell you about Nash? Let him protect you. Then you won't have to worry about invoicing Hades."

Lila lifted the bag of vegetables off her head and scowled. "Message received. Is the lecture over now? I have a headache."

"We expect you to take Nash everywhere now, got it?" Amelia fixed Lila with a narrowed gaze. "Lila?"

"Fine." Lila threw the frozen vegetables on the

bakery counter. "Yes. I will take Nash everywhere. Now can you leave me alone?"

Amelia sniffed. "That's the temperamental daughter I know and love." She knelt next to Nash. "Keep an eye on Lila. She's sneaky, so you'll have to pay extra attention, okay?"

Nash whined in response and Amelia patted his head. "He's very worried and promises to take good care of you. *From now on.*"

"You can understand him?" Xandie stood and rubbed Nash on his head until Theo hissed and extended his claws in her direction. "Geez, relax. He's just a puppy."

"He's the size of a small farm animal and eats his weight in red meat. There's nothing adorable about that diabolical hound." Theo arched his back, fur standing on end.

"I could feel his emotion. He's a little too young to communicate yet. That's if he even develops that gift. His father can talk telepathically, but Cerberus can actually speak words. We'll see which way he goes when he's a little older." Amelia stood and dusted her hands off. "Right, I have to go. For the sake of my sanity, no more bodies, please. The Harrows are getting a reputation." Amelia breezed out of the bakery kitchen, leaving the door swinging.

"I thought we already had a rep because of Elspeth?" Holly offered.

Holly was the youngest of Lila's cousins. Xandie was the middle one, while Lila lorded it over her cousins as the eldest. All three girls shared the same amber eyes, a Harrow trait, along with brown hair. But other than that, they were completely different in every other aspect. Holly was the shortest, but slim, with straight, brown, chin-length hair. Lila took after her mother with her height, but had plenty of curves and long, curly, brown hair. Xandie, with some curves and shoulder-length brown hair that tended to frizz, fell somewhere between Holly and Lila when it came to height. In her mother's words, Lila, the drama queen, Xandie, the bookworm, and Holly, the quiet, death-obsessed one. A disparate trio bound by Harrow genes and an obsessive need to stick their noses into other people's business.

"Apparently our death count rep is growing." Xandie rolled her eyes. "Don't try and blame me. Catalyst, remember? Bodies find me. The murders want to be solved."

"And me now." Lila dumped the vegetables into the trashcan. "Geri Kerr was a mean old woman, but she was as regular as clockwork with her cupcake order. My bank balance will miss her."

"Do we know what happened to her yet?"

Theo shook his whiskered face. "No investigating, Sherlock Librarian. You have a trip with your mother and Elspeth to Andrews, to see your father, scheduled today. Remember?"

Xandie poked her tongue out at him. "I'll regret every day getting Elspeth to spell your voice for karaoke. Now everyone can hear your lectures. Any idea how many complaints I get about you in a day?"

Elspeth Harrow, grandmother, matriarch of the Harrow family and slightly evil hag, wandered into the bakery kitchen. "It was for the love of karaoke. I stand by my actions. The Titanic song was an epic rendition A platinum blonde wig lay in ringlets down her back."

"Blondes hex it better, I take it?" Lila winked at her grandmother. A certifiable loose cannon with a gift for hexes and meddling, Elspeth didn't do boring. Normally a closed book about her past, they'd found out not so long ago that their grandmother had been a super magic spy during World War Two and the leader of the infamous Morrigan coven. Until they'd disbanded and a killer came hunting Elspeth years later. Her grandmother lost almost all her coven-friends and had taken a while to bounce back. But now, her eldest daughter, Miranda, Xandie's mother, had appeared back in their lives after a twenty-year disappearance. No doubt, having Miranda back helped Elspeth to recover.

"You bet your baker booty, girl." Elspeth flipped a curly lock over a shoulder and fixed Harrow amber eyes on her eldest granddaughter. "Another body?"

"Hey, I stumbled across this one. Someone else bopped me on my noggin. Pure coincidence." Lila grabbed the back of her head and winced. Her headache had lessened, but bongo drums still pounded within.

Elspeth sniffed. "Well, make sure you find out who did it. We have to maintain our street cred."

Holly slid a finger into a bowl of bright pink icing and then licked her digit clean. "You mean avoid the Harrows at all costs or you'll end up on one of our murder must-solve lists?"

"Exactly." Elspeth nodded in satisfaction. "The crew likes hearing about our cases. The excitement keeps their tickers going."

"Crew?"

Lila moved the icing bowl out of Holly's reach. "You so don't need those calories, Death Girl." She turned back to Xandie and answered her question. "Elspeth's been hanging out with the Eternal Springs Retirement Home crowd. Actually, she has a weekly poker game and fleeces them out of their savings. Buchanan refuses to play with her anymore." Buchanan, a Paladin, who'd worked with their grandfather, had stepped in when a killer stalked Elspeth. He'd helped solve the Morrigan Coven murders and stuck around Point Muse to keep an eye on the capricious elder Harrow. He popped in and out of town, always keeping busy on super-secret Paladin projects. Lila had a sneaking suspicion that the two had the same fight-flirting going on as her cousin, Xandie, and her Police Chief boyfriend, Zach Braun. The apple didn't fall far from the Harrow dating tree.

"I can't help it if those old people are suckers. Can we get this road trip started? I ain't getting any younger."

With a weary sigh, Xandie stood. "I can see how the next few days will go. Dad will erupt when he sees Elspeth, and then Mom will defend her, and he'll probably lecture her again on living in Point Muse. Then he'll offer me my old job back at the College again. Maybe we *should* stay home."

"Where's the mayhem in that?" Elspeth cackled and lights fizzled, while cutlery rattled in the drawers.

"Can the hag act, Elspeth." Lila frowned at her

grandmother. The elderly woman played the wicked witch to a tee, but it was hell on electricity bills.

"Don't worry about me. You should concern yourself with what the health department would do if they saw that." Elspeth pointed over Lila's shoulder then grabbed Xandie and towed her out of the kitchen.

Theo, Xandie's black cat Library guardian, trotted behind. Theo a.k.a. Theophilus, a.k.a. ancient Greek teenager, had been trapped in the Great Library of Alexandria when a demon-possessed Julius Caesar firebombed the Library. To protect Theo, the Library turned the teenager into a cat guardian. Now, Xandie was stuck with him.

Remembering Elspeth's words, Lila spun around as a bang sounded behind her.

"This is all Hades' fault."

THREE

"Bags not cleaning that," Holly burst out, then covered her mouth, forcing snorting laughter back.

"*Nash, no,*" Lila wailed. Nash decided to copy Holly and taste the icing. Unfortunately, with only paws, the puppy hadn't been as successful as her cousin.

Nash shook his head and dislodged the bowl, spraying pink icing over the floor and counter. A large dollop dripped over his eye, and another rolled down his muzzle. Whining, Nash tried to brush it off, only to succeed in smearing it over his face so he looked like a painted clown.

Grabbing a wet dishcloth, Lila started forward, but slipped and flew as her foot hit a pile of icing.

She collapsed to the ground, landing on her padded posterior in the middle of a mass of pink icing.

Nash jolted toward her, only to slide until he ended up in Lila's lap, both covered in a pink icing massacre.

"I wish I had a camera. This would make great blackmail material." Holly bent over, giving into whoops of laughter.

"Please don't mention blackmail around me." Zach Braun, Police Chief, bear shifter and Xandie's boyfriend, lounged in the doorway.

Lila wiped a puddle of icing off her cheek. "Be glad Elspeth, Xandie, and Theo aren't here, or you'd never hear the end of it."

Holly sobered enough to stand and rub her aching rib cage.

"So I take it they've already headed off for Miranda's regular visit back to her husband?" the Police Chief said.

Lila accepted another cloth from Holly and wiped Nash down as well as she could.

Holly reached over and snagged the icing-free puppy. She propped him on her hip and stepped out of the icing bomb zone. "Yep, Xandie, Miranda, and Elspeth have already headed out to Andrews College to see her dad."

"Her dad will hate seeing Elspeth. He can't handle the drama." Lila ran a wet cloth over her face and arms as she talked to Xandie's boyfriend. "Apparently, Elspeth decided to go at the last moment. Probably bored."

Braun shuddered. "We all know what happens when Elspeth's bored."

"Someone ends up dead." Holly giggled, then looked shocked. "I didn't mean it the way it sounded. I'm sure Elspeth isn't involved in any recent murder."

Lila moved away from the mess on the floor. Thankfully she kept a change of clothing in her office for bakery-related emergencies. "Are you checking up on Xandie or is there a purpose to your visit?"

Braun cleared his throat. "Official visit after finding a dead body. I'm just making sure the Harrows aren't nosing around my investigation for once."

"We're always nosing around. Normally you use it as an excuse to flirt with Xandie." *At least Xandie had prospects.* All Lila had was Nash, her hellhound puppy, and a swimming pool of icing mixture. Lila gestured to the mess on the floor. "I have to get this cleaned up. Is there something I can do for you, Chief Braun?"

"I've got your statement from the hospital, I wanted to know if you'd remembered anything else?"

Poor Geri. The icing incident had taken her mind off the woman's murder.

Holly held up a quiet Nash. "I'll take the dog for a toilet trip outside." She placed Nash down on the floor and let him out the back door into the alley.

"Can I clean and talk?"

Braun nodded. "Go ahead."

Lila grabbed a mob and swiftly set her kitchen to rights. "I don't remember much else. I had Geri's regular delivery with me, and I thought it weird no one answered in her shop. Then I pretty much fell over her and someone bopped me on the back of my head." Lila shrugged and stashed her mop away, the kitchen back to its pristine normal self.

"Geri didn't say anything to you?"

"Only that it was too late. Guess she meant too late to escape, or to save her."

"Did you see anything unusual in or outside the shop?"

"I nearly ran two little old ladies over just before I parked. I haven't seen them before in town. As for Geri's shop, everything looked the same to me." Lila tapped her icing-free chin with two fingers, going over her memories of the last few moments before blacking out. "I think a few things may have been moved around, but it's hard to tell since the shop is always such a mess."

"That's what I thought. Did you know anything about Ms. Kerr's next of kin?"

"She didn't talk much about her family. I think she had a couple of sisters, but I had the impression they were estranged or had passed away. That's all I know, sorry."

Braun sighed. "Not much to go on, but it was definitely murder. Blunt instrument to her skull. We found a stuffed weasel next to her. It has traces of blood on it. We're assuming that's the murder weapon. Do you know if she had any enemies?"

Lila scoffed. "Not quite as many as Elspeth, but close. But if you're asking if I had a motive, you can cross me off your list. She was a regular cupcake devourer and my profit margin is in mourning right now. She was worth more to me alive than dead."

"Considering the Harrows' bad habit of getting involved in murder investigations, I wanted to get the warning out of the way first." He frowned and eyeballed Lila. "Hear me, Harrow. Stay out of my investigation."

"Whoa there, bad boy. I'm not Xandie, obsessed with clues, or Holly, in love with the macabre. I bake. I can guarantee you I'm staying as far away from murder as I can. Besides, I've now been informed that a bigwig Boston company hired Elspeth's spare apartment for some old guy while he works in town. Between him, Nash, and the bakery, my time is all used up."

"See that it stays that way."

Lila rolled her eyes. "I'll let you know when Xandie gets back, then you can ambush her with coffee and a lecture wedged in around a murder investigation, okay?" Lila put her hands out and shoved Zach Braun from her kitchen into the shop, and right into mayhem.

A line two people wide snaked from the counter out the door of the bakery. The level of noise had risen to a glass-shattering commotion and Lila's new employee, Janie Preston, had a red flush and a deer-in-the-headlights expression.

"Oi," Lila raised her voice over the crowd's din. "If you want feeding, quiet down."

The crowd of food-loving Point Muse residents toned it down to a low murmur. Sighing in relief, Lila turned to Janie. "What happened? Looks like we had a crowd explosion in here. It was quiet when I headed back to the kitchen."

Janie ran a hand through her short hair. "They piled in. I thought I could handle it, but they kept coming and they all wanted to chat with you."

Lila's bakery Brownie, Hester, slammed another order from her notepad onto the bench. "Done with your rest out the back?"

"Hester," Lila protested. "Someone bopped me on the head yesterday. Cut me some slack."

"The only slacker here is the bakery owner. Now get out there." The Brownie shoved past Lila and headed for the kitchen to perform Brownie magic.

"Fine." Lila gave Janie a quick once-over. The girl's pixie-cut black hair lay plastered against her head with sweat and her face now gleamed with beads of moisture. Poor kid, she'd only worked for Lila for a month. *Talk about a baptism of fire.* "Janie, Hester will let you know when an order is ready for you to grab. Holly should be back with Nash in a moment, and she can help me with the orders as well. Got it?"

Janie nodded convulsively and headed to the kitchen when Hester bellowed for her.

Lila turned back to her line-up of customers. "Right, who's next?"

"That would be me, dear." Winifred Harrow beamed widely at her niece. "How are you feeling?" She leaned forward and lowered her voice. "You know, since your tragic encounter."

"Someone knocked me out after they murdered Geri. It wasn't an encounter. More like assault and murder."

"Murder? Another one?" Es Penne, teenage Dragon and sometimes waitress at the bakery, popped her head around her cousin, Priss Makepeace. "Seriously? You Harrows must be cursed."

"You said it," Lila muttered under her breath.

Priss offered a commiserating smile. "The Academy has me part time, but if you need any help..." She trailed off and winked at Lila

"Baker, remember?" Priss was a human-Dragon mix, and Xandie, Lila, and Holly had helped their new friend when she'd been framed for the murder of a Dragon cousin. It all worked out in the end, and now her newly found grandmother had welcomed Priss into the powerful Penne Drakon clan. Anyone looking at the muscled, blonde-ringleted, bouncy young woman would've thought cheerleader, not a hybrid Dragon fencing master.

"She means in the murder investigation. Not the

bakery. *Murder,*" Es butted in again, with a toss of her silver-streaked, black hair.

Lila shook her head. "Nope. No investigation. I promised Braun."

"We'll see how long that promise lasts for." Holly stepped up next to Priss, a wiggling Nash in her arms.

"I'm not getting involved. I swear it. Now can we focus on food, otherwise there might be riot?" Lila served the dragons then swiftly moved through the line. Janie dashed in and out with the food. Thankfully, most people took the food to go.

Holly leaned against the counter as the crowd dwindled away to only a few people left in the store. "That rush normal?"

"Is after a murder. People in this town are massive gossips." Lila shrugged. "But it all helps my bottom line. I just wish murder didn't have to occur first." Frowning, Lila looked around the bakery. "Where did you end up leaving Nash?"

"Your mom popped in a few seconds ago and took him off on her rounds. She figured while you're surrounded by people at the bakery you should be safe. She'll drop him back later."

"Thank goodness, he'd probably growl and send all my customers running."

"Or eat all your cupcakes," Holly snickered.

Lila glanced around the bakery. Hester, her Brownie employee, cleaned tables, but Janie had disappeared.

"Seen Janie?"

Holly nodded. "I saw her disappear into the kitchen when the crowd thinned out."

Kitchen? "The girl's supposed to be cleaning tables now." Lila opened the door to her kitchen and peered in. Deserted. Either her new employee had disappeared out into the alley for a break or had entered Lila's pantry. New employees were strictly forbidden to set foot in the pantry. Filled with supplies, but also her premade mixes for cakes and slices. Her Decadent Death by Chocolate Brownie mix was one of her best-selling baked goods. Customers and competitors had tried to beg, borrow, and steal her recipe for years. Lila kept the mix under lock and key and the recipe only existed in her mind. The one ingredient that made the mix taste out of this world was her witchy Harrow gift. Pure Harrow magic went into the brownies. And no one could replicate that.

"Janie? You there?" Lila called out and winced as something smashed in her pantry. She wrenched the door open and exposed a guilty-looking Janie with a smashed glass container at her feet.

"Why are you in here? You know you aren't allowed in the pantry without permission."

Janie dropped to the ground, trying to gather the shards of glass together. "I'm sorry, Lila. Since we had such a rush of customers, I thought I'd get some of the mixes out and get ready for you to bake."

"If you need access to my pantry, you ask Hester or myself. Otherwise stay out... *Please.*"

Janie looked at Lila, her face crinkled, and tears dropped. "It's all my fault," she wailed. Standing, Janie dumped a handful of glass into the trashcan and wrapped her arms around her waist. She shot a mournful glance at Lila from tear-drenched eyes. "I won't do it again. I swear." She hiccupped before descending into another round of loud wailing.

"Geez, you're a hard boss. Elspeth never reduced an employee to hysterical crying before." Holly leaned against the open kitchen door.

"The pantry is off-limits. I made that quite clear when I hired her." Lila rolled her eyes. "And Elspeth doesn't have employees."

"You do, and she's still leaking waterworks in your pantry."

Janie broke the rules and she was the bad guy?

"Fine." Lila grabbed Janie and moved her onto a stool in the kitchen. "Look, it's okay. Just don't do it again. If you want to help, ask Hester or myself next time."

Gulping, Janie's wailing eased until she uttered only the odd sniff. "Thank you, Lila. I swear it won't happen again. Promise."

A nice girl, but so clumsy and prone to sudden bouts of tears. Lila couldn't count the number of ruined dishes and broken plates they'd gone through in the last month. But everyone had to start somewhere, and as long as sorties into her pantry stopped, Lila was willing to forget. She forced a smile. "It's fine, now head out the front and see if Hester has anything for you to do."

Nodding, Janie stood and rushed out, leaving an exhausted Lila in her wake.

"Man, I'd hate it if you were my boss." Holly inclined her head and studied her cousin. "Close the bakery for the rest of the day and we'll go collect Nash."

Lila sighed and agreed. "I'm glad to see this day finished. Between the murder, my head injury, and the bakery rush, I'm done. Dipped in sugar, deep-fried, and completely done."

The trill of an Elspeth-spelled phone cut into the kitchen calm.

"Please don't let that be another dead body."

Lila shushed her cousin and answered, "Heart's Delight Bakery, Lila Harrow speaking."

"The talented Lila Harrow, owner and baker. Lovely to finally speak to you."

A woman's plummy tones filtered down the phone line with haughtiness and condescension. Must be one of Elspeth's enemies. "What can I do for you?"

"Why, sell me your Decadent Death by Chocolate Brownie recipe, of course. I hear it truly is to die for." The woman trilled a high-pitched laugh.

Again? Maybe it was time to retire her best-selling recipe. The unending phone calls from different people demanding the recipe had become annoying. "Whoever you are, the recipe isn't for sale."

"Oh gosh, silly me. My name's Marie Hestis. I'm an employee of Hestia Wholesome Hits. And I'll pay anything for that brownie recipe."

Great! Hestia Wholesome Hits, formed by the Greek Goddess of hearth and home, Hestia, and now run by descendants, had hounded her for the brownie recipe for the last year. Frankly, it was ironic because the Goddess was supposed to be a virgin. *Whatever.* However, this brownie groupie wasn't getting her hand on Lila's baked goods. "The answer is no, not in my lifetime," Lila spat the words into the phone.

"You should rethink your position, Ms. Harrow."

"And why would that be?"

"Because from what I hear, you have a murder issue on your hands."

What? How could the woman have heard about the murder? And what did that have to do with her bakery? Or her brownie recipe? "What makes you say that?"

"Because I hear the body and your cupcakes were found together. Not great business practice."

"I went there to deliver a cupcake order. Then someone attacked me. That's nothing to do with my food."

"Wouldn't take much for people to connect your food to murder. Bad publicity affects the bottom line in our business."

"Why you..." Words failed Lila at the woman's nasty implications.

"Now, now. All I'm saying is it would be beneficial for you if you accepted our offer. Otherwise, you never know what might happen to your business. Think about it."

The woman hung up, leaving Lila gaping at the phone.

"What was all that about?" Holly frowned at Lila as she tossed the phone across the room with a screech.

Lila pointed a dramatic finger at the now shattered phone. "That was a snake in the grass and sadly my wake-up call."

"Huh?"

"I don't have a choice now. I have to solve Geri's death and make sure my bakery's name stays out of the murder business."

"Finally." Holly clapped. "What do we do first?"

Lila smiled slowly. "First step? Breaking and entering."

Time to channel her cousin, Xandie, and Sherlock up.

FOUR

"I thought you said you had it handled?"

"I said I had a handle. This one." Holly held up an emerald-green handle with silver grooves etched around it.

"What good is a handle? We need a lock pick or a skeleton key."

Both cousins shuddered.

The last time they needed a skeleton key, Elspeth had come through all right, with a skeleton key carved from a finger bone from her great aunt Rose. Xandie had remained traumatized and refused to even mention the phrase skeleton key. Lila grimaced in solidarity with her murder-solving cousin. "How's your handle going to help us now?"

"You're supposed to attach a lock pick to the end

and then it magically drills the lock and *abracadabra,* you're breaking and entering."

"Where's the lock pick?"

Holly rolled her eyes. "That's what I'm telling you. I bought the magic handle. You were supposed to bring the lock pick."

Lila stared baffled at her cousin. Supposedly the calm, think-every-move-through kind of girl, instead, Holly seemed to get battier by the second.

Holly defended herself. "At least I thought of this." She waggled the green stick at Lila. "I just naturally assumed you'd be contributing to our breaking and entering plan."

"You know what they say about assume."

"What?"

"It makes an ass out of you and me."

"*Really?* Do they really say that? Or is it just you trying to be smart?" Holly frowned. "For that matter, who are *they?*"

Lila banged her head against the shop's back door. She needed to find Geri's killer and clear her bakery's reputation, but did she really have to be saddled with her cousin, Holly?

"This might help." A thin silver claw appeared in front of Lila.

Squinting, Lila angled the flashlight behind her

and outlined Priss Makepeace in its muted glow. Silvery eyes with vertical slits for pupils blinked myopically for a moment before morphing back into human-looking cornflower blue eyes. Okay, technically she didn't need the flashlight since full dark hadn't set yet. But it made her feel super thief to flash one around...*pun intended.*

"Holly forgot the lock pick."

"Hey. I told you. You were supposed to bring it, not me. Handle, remember?"

"Remember assume?" Lila snapped.

"Like I said, not a problem." Priss inserted her claw into the door lock and jiggled it slightly until it clicked. "Have Dragon claw. Can lock pick." Priss opened the door and scooted in a few paces before calling all clear softly.

Holly sniffed and shoved her magic handle in the back pocket of her black jeans. Ignoring the still-kneeling Lila, she shoved past her cousin into the darkened shop.

Seriously? Family was so much work. Lila moved to push up from the ground but froze as someone breathed heavily in her ear. She turned her head and met the faint red glowing eyes of her ferocious hellhound puppy, Nash. "We left you with my mother. Don't tell me you broke another window? I'm not sure how many that penny pincher Hades will fork out for."

Nash panted, tongue out, then leaned in and dropped a slobbery kiss on Lila's cheek.

Wiping the rivulet of drool, she pointed a finger at her four-legged bodyguard. "Okay, you can stay but only if you do what I say. And if you get a chance to pee on Holly... *Take it*. She needs bringing down a peg or two." Lila stood and dusted her jeans.

"Yoo hoo, Lila, dear?" A plump, middle-aged lady with flaming red hair stood behind a dingy gray picket fence diagonally across from the back of Geri 's shop.

Lila forced a smile and spun, one hand on Nash's collar so he didn't charge off. "Hi, Susie, what can I do for you?" Please don't say you've called the cops because you spotted the Harrows breaking and entering. Henrietta Barnes' house sat by itself diagonally across from Geri's shop and with Hetty in the retirement village, Lila had thought they could sneak in without being spied on.

Susie tittered. "It's what I can do for you, Lila. Mother would love to have a word with you about a regular cupcake delivery. She's completely obsessed with your vanilla Viagra for the Soul cupcakes. They really give her a get up and go."

Susie's mother, Henrietta Barnes, was a permanent Resident of Eternal Springs Retirement Home, so get up and go might be appropriate. "Of course. I'm happy to work in a regular delivery for her."

"She really wants to speak to you about something else important as well." Susie pouted. "She won't even tell me what it's about."

Susie might look harmless but inside her fluffy exterior beat the heart of a barracuda gossip. Henrietta not divulging why she wanted Lila to visit must be killing her daughter inside. Lila raised her voice. "I'll check in with Henrietta tomorrow. I'm a little tied up right now." Or she would be if anyone found out from Susie that Lila had broken into Geri's shop.

"Poor Geri. I know you two were close, but she really was a horrid woman. She used to leave her trashcans piled up behind the shop until collection day. The mess drove my mother crazy." She eyed Lila and Nash and the open shop door. "Did she leave you the shop?"

Running Geri's Trash and Curio Store was not on this little baker girl's cards. Lila shook her head. "I left my best cupcake platter inside. Since Geri gave me her keys as a backup ages ago, I thought I'd grab it before the shop goes to her heirs."

The green-eyed monster disappeared from Susie's eyes and she deflated. "Oh, makes sense. Don't forget to go see Mother. I'm sure it's nothing important, but it will put an old woman's mind at rest." Susie winked and sauntered back inside her mother's cottage.

"Meddling Susie will be on a gossip warpath until she finds out what her mother wants with me. Just perfect." Lila pushed Nash into Geri's shop then closed the door behind him as he trotted across to join Holly and Priss.

Holly tapped her foot on the floor. "What took so long? Time waits for no break and enterer..." She cocked her head. "Okay, that's not exactly a word, but you get my drift."

"Susie Barnes is what happened."

"Oh great. Braun will be here any minute with the way that woman spreads gossip." Holly raised her hands into the air in a non-verbal statement and stomped past Lila to the back door. "We need to get out of here before he finds us."

"And they call me a drama llama." Lila grabbed Holly by the shoulders and steered her back towards Priss. "Relax, worrywart. Her Mom wants to talk to me, and she passed on the message. I told her I had Geri's backup key and just wanted to pick up my cupcake tray. So, we have to be quick or she'll get suspicious and blab to Braun."

Both girls stared at Lila, then around the trash and treasure labyrinth of the Curio Shop.

"What are you doing? Get to it."

Holly pointed at Nash. "Amelia will have a few words about you leaving him behind again and him taking off."

"Whatever. Let's get sleuthing before we get caught. Look for anything that's out of place."

Priss played the beam of her flashlight over the crowded shop. "How could you tell? This place is a hoarder's delight."

Lila ran her eyes over a stuffed moose, a child's rusty red bike, and overflowing shelves of valuable '*trash*'. "Geri had a few issues with letting go of her collection, but oddly enough, she had collectors from all over contacting her. Most of this is rubbish, but she'd find the odd diamond in the rough sometimes."

"She was mean. Meaner than my grandmother and Elspeth put together." Priss grimaced when she knocked over a moth-eaten stuffed monkey with hands over its ears.

"Our grandmothers aren't known for their welcoming manner, but they aren't outright shoot-him-down kind of mean, like Geri."

Lila glared at Holly. "She wasn't that bad, just misunderstood." Lila stomped to where she'd found Geri's body. An outline of her body still remained from the crime scene people, but all Lila's Blue Serenity cupcakes had been taken as evidence. Spinning around, Lila squinted at the shadowed shop interior. *Nothing seemed out of place.*

"That's horrible." Holly fake-gagged and shone her flashlight again on a large dusty painting that sat propped up against the back wall.

Priss and Lila followed the light until they stood next to Holly.

A dark and gloomy battle scene featuring ancient Greek warriors dominated the canvas. Looming over the bloodied chest of a fallen warrior were three female death spirits. Stringy long gray hair trailed out behind them. The middle figure held a bronze dagger aloft with a silver glowing ball hovering at the tip of it. The other two spirits each had a clawed hand on the central figure's bony shoulders.

Priss shuddered. "Okay, that's nasty. Looks like they're sucking the poor guy's soul out."

"Actually, they're death Daimons. The Keres, I think." Holly squinted at a tiny, engraved plaque on the frame of the painting. "Yep. Keres sisters. Death spirits, kind of like the Valkyrie but not so nice and busty. The Keres are more drawn to wholesale murder and slaughter. They use the dagger to draw out the souls of the slaughtered and deliver it to Hades."

"Personally, I'd prefer nice and busty to scary and skanky. Hang on." Lila snapped her fingers. "My dad mentioned those Keres women. Apparently two of the old hags escaped Tartarus and Hades. They have a grudge against my dad since he arrested them. That's why he gave me Nash as added protection." Lila stared at the hellhound gnawing on a fuzzy monkey paw. "*Apparently?*"

Priss gave Nash a scratch on the head. "He's cute. I like him."

Holly drew in close to the painting, studying it intently.

Lila frowned. Something had sparked Holly's interest. Maybe her quiet, death-loving cousin had stumbled upon a clue? "Have you found something?"

Pressing her lips, Holly tapped the dagger in the painting. "Maybe... This knife looks awfully familiar somehow. I think I've seen it, or a picture of it, before."

"It's a clue then?" Please let it be a clue. Otherwise, Lila was completely clueless... pun intended.

"I'll have to do some research, but yeah, I think

we found a clue."

Lila whooped and shoved a fist in the air. "I'm so not clueless."

Nash raised his head with a jerk and growled low and long. His teeth reflected in the glow of the flashlight.

Priss pointed at the dog. "Your pet's growling and I'm pretty sure I saw flames in his eyes."

Lila kneeled in front of the hellhound. "Since you're supposed to be my doggy protector, I take it your super underworld senses have picked up something?"

Opening his mouth, he burped flames, which narrowly avoided singeing Lila.

"Great, a dog with acid reflux. My life is complete."

Two high-pitched voices at the unlocked back door of Geri's shop scattered the sleuthing trio.

Lila grabbed Nash and ducked into a shadowed corner behind a freestanding rack of dirty and stained wedding dresses.

Holly ducked behind a large fake, stuffed, woolly mammoth and Priss squeezed behind a cabinet loaded with antique knives of all different sizes.

"What a dump."

"Always a hoarder and not to mention a double-crosser."

"Quite right. And how careless to leave your back door unlocked, but I guess she got hers."

Both women cackled, raucous, grating laughter that ripped at Lila's nerve endings. She eased away from the dresses and peered out. The shop was too dark for Lila to make out any distinguishing features. But the women sounded old and crotchety like Elspeth, only aged another hundred years on top.

"We still need that dagger. Everything is pointless without it. Hades will track us down. Then we're back to that unending horror of a prison again." One of the women slowly turned around. "We just have to think like our oldest sister. The dagger would be somewhere close so she could keep an eye on it, but still gloat about her double-cross at the same time."

"What about that human who found her body? Would our sister have given her the dagger?" As the other woman talked, she moved toward the knife cupboard.

Priss? Lila closed her eyes and gripped Nash's collar tight. Whoever they were, these women had killed Geri and knocked Lila out cold. Who knew what they would do if they found Priss behind the cupboard, spying?

"She's human, our sister wouldn't dare." The other woman clapped her hands, and a weak light illuminated the painting of the Daimons on the battlefield carnage. "Lookee look. What a crafty sister we had." She pointed to the knife held between the three sisters in the painting.

"Hidden in plain sight. A trickster, our eldest sister was." The other woman drew back from the knife cupboard and joined her sister in front of the large painting.

Nash trembled under Lila's hands and jerked as the women cackled and danced in victory.

Lila tightened her hold on the hellhound, but he slipped away and shot straight at the women, howling. She could do nothing but hold her breath and hope they left her demonic puppy alone.

The closer Nash drew to the women the larger he grew. Flames illuminated his eyes and lit the figures.

"Hound," the tallest of the hags screeched. She grabbed a decorated flowerpot and pitched it at the dog's head.

"Damn Hades and his trackers." The other shorter woman grabbed her sister. "It's a puppy, it won't be able to track us too far. We need to get out of here now."

"But the dagger?" her sister wailed, tugging at a sparse gray hair that lay knotted over a peeling scalp.

"We know where it is now. But it's time to depart before we're found out." She dragged her sister to the back door, then peered at the hellhound as it stalked her, smoke trickling from his nostrils. Her mouth hardened into a line of hate. "She won't win, we will be as we once were." With that, the hag slammed the door, just before Nash hit it, headfirst.

Lila scrambled out and ran for Nash. She ran her hands over his body and crooned compliments to the animal. "What a good boy. Who's a good hound? Who's a good fire-belching hellhound?"

Nash burped and green-tinged smoke trickled out of his nostrils.

Holding her nose, Holly scrambled out from behind her woolly mammoth hiding place. "That mammoth stinks like it died yesterday."

"At least we don't smell like that." Lila rubbed Nash's ears again.

"Thanks to your new puppy." Priss let out the breath she'd been holding. "Those old hags sounded nasty."

"And related to Geri. The old women must be Geri's sisters who escaped Hades and Tartarus. The reason the God of the Underworld gave Nash to me."

Both Hades and her father had known Geri was in Point Muse. "This is all Hades' fault. He put Geri here and now we have a murder and demonic jail-birds stalking the place."

"And they're looking for this dagger." Holly tapped the painting and the rune-carved painted dagger in the hands of the Daimons.

Lila slapped Holly's back. "Since we're without our resident researcher and this painting deals with death, you're up. Welcome to the big leagues."

"Is it bad to hope Xandie's reunion gets cut short?" Holly shook her head. "I'll ask my necro-mancer bosses. They might know about the dagger."

"Meanwhile, we need to leave, ASAP. I don't want to spend another night at the Point Muse police station." Priss indicated flashing lights at the front of the store.

Months ago, poor Priss Makepeace had been arrested for the murder of her Dragon cousin, Archibald Penne. Xandie, Lila and Holly managed to prove her innocence, but Priss had a few issues with the Point Muse police force. Now Lila thought about it, she had a few issues with Chief Braun and the police department too... Namely getting caught for breaking and entering.

"Time to jet, sleuthers."

Holly burst into Lila's bakery the next day, chest heaving and her windblown chin-length bob making her look like a crazy woman. "Braun's on the warpath."

Lila smiled at an elderly customer and handed over a takeaway coffee before turning to her cousin. "And? The Police Chief is always on the warpath."

Holly sidled over, grabbed Lila, and dragged her over to the kitchen door. "Not like this. Someone broke into Geri's shop."

"Yeah, we did." Lila rolled her eyes. "Remember last night? Those nasty old women broke in after we did, and Nash burped flames at them?"

Shaking her head furiously, Holly leaned in and whispered, "Someone else broke in after us and trashed the shop." She widened her eyes for impact. "*And* they tore up that painting."

"Okay, so those nasty bats must've come back and decided to redecorate."

"No, no, no." Holly waved her hands around for emphasis. "Think about that painting. The dagger looked so real. I think Geri hid the dagger in the painting and now her sisters have found it. Do you get how bad this is? There had to be a good reason she hid the dagger from them."

Lila slapped her palm on her forehead. "Hecate's toenails, I didn't make the connection and we don't know enough about the dagger to know what their next step is. *Or* how bad the fallout is." Lila rubbed her chin, thoughtfully. The dagger was important. She could feel it in her baker bones. She pointed a finger at Holly. "We need information. Get research-ing, Xandie clone."

"I'll speak to my bosses later; they might have some ideas. Meanwhile, avoid Braun, he'll probably blame us."

A deep voice boomed behind her. "Yes, I will. So why don't you tell me the truth right now?"

The Harrow bad luck strikes again. Lila spun around and faced Police Chief Zach Braun. "Fine. We searched Geri's place for clues, but we had a key.

Which isn't breaking and entering. *And* we didn't trash the place."

"I know." Braun smirked. "A witness spotted you three sneaking out and then the two old women smashed in the back door after you'd gone. I just wanted to know if you'd tell me the truth."

Lila whacked Braun's meaty arm. "You have an evil streak, Zach. You should've been born a Harrow. Holly might've had a nervous breakdown. You know what she's like."

Nibbling on a nail, Holly pulled a face as they both stared at her. "I'm not going to melt into a witchy banshee puddle. I just get anxious."

Lila turned back to Braun. "Ignore her. I take it Susie couldn't help watching the drama unfold?"

"I can neither confirm nor deny that Susie Barnes is the witness. But off the record? She confirmed your story. Do you know anything about those old women?"

"I think they're related to Geri. Sisters. My dad told me they escaped from Tartarus. Geri turned on them and Hades gave her witness protection in Point Muse. The hags are some kind of Daimon who suck souls for Hades. Until the three of them went on strike. That's all I know."

"Keep an eye out. If you see anything, you let me know." Braun raised an eyebrow. "Got it?"

Lila waved at Braun. "Whatever, lawman. I have a business to run so skedaddle."

Tipping an imaginary hat, Braun sauntered off.

"So, we're looking for two desiccated old murderous women who like creepy daggers?"

Lila pointed a finger at Holly. "Correct and you're leaving to research right now." A loud clang of something metallic hitting the floor, accompanied by shriek from the kitchen, had Lila wincing.

Holly sidled away. "Sounds like you're busy. Have fun." She waved and bolted out the door.

Everyone's a comedian. Lila pushed her kitchen door open and froze at the mess. "What did you do this time, Janie?"

Lila's bakery assistant stood wringing her hands in the middle of a flood of cupcake batter.

"I carried the batter to the fridge, just like you asked. But the bowls slipped out of my arms."

Talk about a walking jinx. Everything Janie touched ended up with Lila going full cleaner on her kitchen. "Did you try and carry all the bowls together?"

Janie nodded and covered her face with her hands, wailing like the banshee she wasn't. "I thought I'd save time." She peeked between her fingers at Lila and her sobbing increased in tempo.

The kitchen door thumped open behind her, and Nash galloped in, knocking Lila to her knees. Her hands flailed on the floor as she catapulted forward into the cupcake batter. Nash slid past Janie and slammed into the firewall with a thunk.

With a sigh, Lila leveraged herself up. "At least I have an apron on this time."

"I'm such a klutz, Lila. I'm really sorry."

For someone who'd been wailing up a river, Janie looked remarkably put together. "Don't worry about the cupcake batter. Get the new load of brownies out. I already have the Eternal Springs order ready to go. I'll take Nash and do the delivery. Hester's in charge while I'm away, follow whatever she says."

The Brownie popped her head into the kitchen. "Then I say it's time for a raise."

Lila yanked her apron off and grabbed a box of cupcakes. "You get a raise when I do. Which is never considering the rate we're going." Whistling for Nash, who was now licking the floor with his wide, slobbery tongue, Lila turned to Janie. "Please, clear this mess up. And take a breath and slow down." With a wave, Lila ducked out to the alley behind her bakery and her waiting luminescent blue bakery van.

At least she'd managed to escape the batter chaos for the retired Point Muse residents clamoring for her cupcakes. The silver lining in her day.

"Really, here? It smells like death and old people."

"Perfect for us then." The older woman, who looked to be in her sixties, cackled and nudged another woman around a similar age.

Lila paused a moment and juggled her carton of cupcakes. She frowned. Something about the two women seemed vaguely familiar. She stared at them and shook her head. No, not anyone she knew, despite the feeling of familiarity.

She turned her attention back to the matter at hand. Nash had already bounded off, heading for the kitchen and a dog treat from the head witch chef. The elderly residents of Eternal Springs Retirement Village loved visiting with playful animals. The hellhound would fit right in. Janie had delivered a load of cupcakes yesterday for a party, so Lila's order today was just a top up. Plus, it meant she could drop in on Henrietta, a.k.a. Hetty Barnes, and see what the woman wanted. Hetty was just as much a gossip queen as her daughter, Susie.

"I don't know how humans do it. Packed in here like rotting sardines. Give me fragrant blood-soaked meadows any day."

"Shush. Incognito, remember?" The shorter woman grabbed her friend and yanked her to the side.

Point Muse just got weirder. Lila kept her gaze zeroed in on her box of baked goods as she shuffled past. She headed for the nurse's station, leaving the two women whispering fiercely behind her.

"Lila, I'm so glad to see you." A younger woman with a bright blue pixie cut rushed up and almost yanked the box of cupcakes out of the baker's grasp in her excitement.

"Excited much? Didn't Janie drop some cupcakes over yesterday?"

"She did and made a big effort to get around and talk to all of our residents, especially some of our more long-term ones. But you know how much the hoard loves your food. Always puts them in a good mood."

"Good to know." Lila winked at Ellie. She'd wondered why Janie had taken so long. The girl seemed twitchy when she'd come back from the retirement home. Maybe the oldies had exhausted her assistant.

"Is it okay if I visit Hetty? Susie said she'd asked after me."

"Sure, no worries. You know where her room is." Ellie nodded to Lila and scooted off with the box of goodies. She spun around after a few steps. "Try and get her to have a rest. She's been quite popular. The last visitor only left a few minutes ago."

"At least someone has a social life."

"You and me both. This job is full on, and I get called in at all hours. Helping people is worth it, though."

As a healer, Ellie couldn't help herself. Her gift flared into action as soon as someone ill or injured crossed her radar.

Ellie frowned. "I'm glad you're visiting Hetty today. She's been unsettled. Something made her anxious and she won't talk to anyone but you. Even Susie couldn't get it out of her. And boy, was Susie unimpressed."

"The gossip queen herself couldn't pry a juicy story out of her own mother? That would have fried Susie's gossip nerves."

"Just a tad. Hetty had a day release at home, but once she arrived back and after Janie's visit, she started getting anxious. But you're here now." Ellie winked and sauntered back down the hallway with the cupcakes.

What happened after Janie's visit? Or did Janie upset Hetty? That girl certainly upset Lila's batter more than once.

A flash of black shot up next to Lila, almost tripping her. "Nash, slow down." Her excited hellhound panted and cocked his head as if processing her words.

Making sure no one saw her, Lila leaned down and brushed a kiss on the gangly puppy's head. "Don't want anyone thinking I'm soft on you. But you *are* cute." She scratched his ears and carried on into Hetty's room. She'd been here a few times to drop cupcakes off to the elderly woman. The old girl had a powerful sweet tooth...

Lila stopped suddenly as she realized the door to the room stood partially ajar. She frowned. That wasn't normal for the retirement village. A kernel of worry wormed its way into her brain. Before she could act on it, Nash cannonballed into Lila's legs and sent her flying into Hetty's room, surprising a large behemoth of a man hunched over the still body of Henrietta Barnes.

Lila let out a bloodcurdling scream and Nash

leapt forward, growling, his teeth bared and eyes aflame.

"Whoa there. Calm down, especially you, hellhound." The man stepped away from the old woman's body, hands up in the air.

"Who are you and what have you done? What's wrong with Hetty?"

"She's dead," he responded.

Lila gaped and pointed a finger at him. "You? *You* killed Hetty Barnes? How could you? Why? She loved my cupcakes. I can't afford to have another regular cupcake customer murdered."

"Maybe she loved your cupcake a little too much, considering she choked on it."

"*What,*" Lila screeched. "There's no way that could have happened. My cupcakes are as light as air and melt in your mouth."

"If she were alive, I'm pretty sure the old girl wouldn't agree with you."

"Nash, keep him still." Lila poked her head out into the hallway and hollered, "Code red. Code red. Someone get Braun. Hetty's been murdered." Lila turned back to the cupcake hater. He didn't really look like a shifty-eyed murderer. With dark black hair, gray eyes, and a big beak nose only a mother could love, he looked menacing enough, just not a steely-eyed killer. "Why did you kill her?"

The guy sighed and ran his hand through his head. "I told you. I didn't. But the cupcake shoved in her mouth probably did."

"No," Lila wailed and stepped around the bed to the other side. Murder suspect number one was right. Wedged into Hetty's throat was a Vanilla Viagra for the Soul cupcake. She'd probably suffocated from the obstruction. But something else niggled at Lila. She pointed to a small cross someone had cut into Hetty's open palm. "Why did you cut her hand like that?"

The man jerked and went over the bed. "Damn." He immediately grabbed his phone and tapped out a text.

"You have time to text, killer?"

He gritted his teeth. "My name isn't murderer or killer, it's Matthew. And the murder is over. She's dead and I didn't kill her, your cupcakes did."

Lila reared back, her gasp of indignation rocking the room. "How dare you. My cupcakes are murder free. It's a guarantee."

"She obviously didn't get that memo." Matthew shrugged his wide shoulders.

Lila stood at five feet seven inches and the killer

named Matthew still dwarfed her. Even Zach Braun, Police Chief, and bear shifter, would have issues taking this guy down. Speaking of Braun, shouldn't he be here by now?

Right on cue, Braun rushed in, weapon drawn. Bear hump and a monobrow formed as he took in the room at a glance. Behind him hovered numerous members of the nursing staff and a handful of residents. He waved one of the nurses into the room to check Hetty's vitals then shooed her out, closing the door on the rest of the staff and residents. He holstered his weapon and the hump, and the eyebrow, shrank to normal proportions. "Another one, Matthew?" he asked.

The other man nodded and shook Braun's hand. "Looks like it, Zach. Sorry it's in your jurisdiction now. You open to a joint investigation?"

"Happy to help the company any time. Got any ideas?"

Matthew pointed to an open-mouth Lila. "I give you suspect number one. Death by cupcake."

Braun closed his eyes. "What is it with you Harrows and dead bodies?"

"She's done this before?" Matthew growled in Lila's direction.

"The whole family leaves a trail of bodies behind them."

"Zach Braun, you're a dead man," Lila spat out.

Braun kneeled next to Nash and whispered into his ear for a moment.

The hellhound whimpered and lay on the ground, paws over his eyes.

Matthew stepped over to Lila and pulled her arms gently behind her, cuffing them. "Law enforcement doesn't appreciate death threats."

Lila screeched, "You're both going to pay for this."

Braun smiled wearily at the warring duo. "Matthew Grim, meet your landlady."

Lila's screech carried down the hallway as her new tenant hauled her away.

SIX

"I didn't kill her. I told you. My cupcakes are murder free. Aren't you listening to me?" Lila grouched at the two men interrogating her.

"Henrietta Barnes died with one of your cupcakes stuck in her throat. That makes you a suspect." Matthew Grim leaned back in his police issue metal chair and smirked at Lila.

"Smug Scandinavian skipping skunk." Lila rattled her chains on the table before turning to the police chief. "And you, traitor, don't think I won't tell Xandie everything. You'll end up as a bearskin rug on Elspeth's bedroom floor."

Braun shuddered. "The less I remember about Elspeth's bedroom, the better. Just answer our questions, Lila. It's important."

Ignoring the Benedict Arnold of bear shifters, Lila ranted, "And to think we opened our arms and gathered you to the collected bosoms of the Harrow family. We even hid you from your very own murder charge, or don't you remember Colin and that cupboard in Elspeth's room?"

"*Argh.*" Braun lowered his head to the table, banging it hard a few times as he mumbled something.

"Excuse me? I don't speak soon-to-be-hexed speech. I'm betting Elspeth's on her way with Xandie and her gun-toting, black-ops specialist mother right now. Elspeth can always sense when carnage is going down." Lila scrutinized her short nails before looking up and smiling sweetly. "I wouldn't want to be you two," she sang.

"You letting her get away with all that drivel?" Matthew Grim shook his head. "You're getting soft, Braun. Heard you'd settled down with the Librarian. Maybe Point Muse is too quiet. You need the challenge of the big smoke."

Braun gurgled and slumped back into his chair. "For the love of everyone's sanity, Lila. Just tell me what you saw. That's all I need. Please."

She did kind of feel bad for Xandie's boyfriend,

but the fiend next to him burned her sugar and soured her milk. Lila couldn't think of anything else but the fact she really wanted to wipe Matthew Grim's smirk right off that not-at-all appealing mug. But for the sake of her cousin Xandie's non-single status, she could afford to throw the bear shifter a bone. "Since Chief Braun is my designated law enforcement representative, I'll happily divulge my witness statement. But not in front of the murderous interloper who has a creepy hold over the Chief." Lila grinned her victory.

Grim slapped the table and spoke through gritted teeth. "I. Did. Not. Kill. Henrietta. Barnes."

"You say potato..." Lila shrugged, unconcerned, and bit back a smile as the other man ground his teeth. There was a remarkably large amount of satisfaction to be found in annoying an uptight man.

"Lila, I've known Matthew and his family for years."

"Do tell, Police Chief Braun?"

"The Grim family are reapers. They run Grim Inc. They collect souls and deliver them to their final resting place. When supernatural law enforcement has a soul-related death issue, Grim Inc. gets called in. I've worked with Matthew before." Braun leaned forward. "You can trust him. But we need to know what you saw."

Lila tapped the table thoughtfully and stared at her hellhound. Her protective puppy had passed out in the corner of the interrogation room, obviously not worried about her safety. Maybe she should take a cue from him. "This is about Geri and her sisters, isn't it?"

Braun and Grim shared a look, then the reaper took the lead. "Care to tell me why you connect the murder to Geri Kerr and her sisters?"

"Because I caught my father canoodling with my mother, and he forced a hellhound puppy on me for protection from those same sisters." Lila jerked a thumb over her shoulder at the snoring hound. "Yeah, he's totally protecting me."

Braun leaned forward, worry lining his forehead. "This is serious. We need to know what's going on."

"All Dad told me is that the Keres sisters broke out of Tartarus. Since he imprisoned them both, Hades and Dad think they might land here in Point Muse for revenge against the family.

"And you were friends with Geri Kerr?"

"A client. Geri loved my cupcakes. I supplied regular deliveries to her. Not a friend."

"And you supplied cupcakes to Henrietta Barnes as well?"

"I didn't kill her. I didn't kill either Geri *or* Hetty. I just delivered cupcakes."

"And yet I found Henrietta Barnes with one of your cupcakes wedged in her throat."

Lila groaned. "The only reason I turned up with cupcakes was that I got wind that Hetty needed to talk to me. I didn't kill her. Besides, I saw *you* standing over her body."

"I'm a reaper, I guide people's souls to wherever they're supposed to be, I don't kill them first."

"*Ha!* How do I know that?" Lila shook her head and speared Grim with a sneering look. "Where's your sharp stick thing. Every picture you see of the Grim Reaper, they have a sharp thingy in their hands."

"It's a scythe. Not stick thingy." Grim massaged his head. "And I didn't have it out because her soul had already departed before I arrived."

"Don't you carry it everywhere? Just in case?" Lila frowned. "How do you carry it around in public? Kind of a giveaway as to what you do. Pretty big."

Matthew sighed and took a small pen-sized object out of his pocket. "Happy? That's my scythe. Can we get back to what you saw now?"

Lila pursed her lips. "I would think size would matter."

Matthew shoved his scythe back in his pocket. "It's not the size that matters, but the will of the person who uses it. Plus, it changes sizes as needed. Can we get back on target?"

"Wow, sensitive much?" Lila mumbled and resisted the urge to cackle like Elspeth as she needled the reaper. "Geri's door was open when I brought the cupcakes over. I stumbled over a body, and someone bopped me over the head. That's it."

Braun nodded. "That matches with your original statement. But what about Hetty?"

"Like I said, Hetty needed to talk to me. I thought I'd drop a cupcake order off at the same time. I talked to one of the nurses and handed off my cupcakes to her. Then I headed to Hetty's room and found the Grim Reaper looming over her dead body."

Braun forestalled Matthew's protest with a sharp motion of his hand.

"Did you see anyone strange going to Hetty's room?"

Had she? Everything seemed normal at the retirement home except those two old women she'd almost run into... "I saw two old women visiting the home."

Matthew leaned forward, eyes focused on Lila. "What's so strange about two women visiting other old people in a home? What made you notice them?"

"Now I put my mind to it, I think maybe they were the same women I nearly ran into in my van just before I headed into Geri's shop. They didn't look quite so haggy at the retirement home, but their features were the same."

"You saw them just before you broke into Ms. Kerr's shop?"

"Now, Chief. You know I'd never break into anyone's shop. I had a key." She smirked at the law enforcement duo.

"A key called Priss and her Dragon claws. So, you saw the women, what then?"

"The three of us were looking around when we heard someone coming in, so we hid."

Matthew raised an eyebrow. "Three?"

Braun cleared his throat. "There's another Harrow cousin, Holly. She's part banshee and works at the Elysian Fields Mortuary and Cemetery. Now keep going, Lila."

"We hid, they busted in looking for something and Nash scared them off. That's all."

"What were these women looking for?"

"A dagger we think. Holly's researching it with her bosses."

Braun nodded and raised an eyebrow at the reaper.

Matthew agreed with a nod. "It's probably them."

"Them who?"

"The Keres Daimons. Geri Kerr was a triplet demon. The three death Daimons collected souls for Hades."

"Dad already told me about them. How about you release me if that's all you needed?" Lila rattled the spelled cuffs.

"We found an X carved into Hetty's hand. Those two old women you saw on the road, then breaking into Geri's shop, and again at the retirement home, were likely to be Geri's sisters."

"But the two women I saw outside the retirement home were younger. They definitely had more hair."

Matthew nodded. "That sounds about right. Every time they take a soul with the dagger of Degmon, it rejuvenates them. It's an effect of the dagger which wears off after they deliver the soul to Hades. Hades would allow them to keep a portion of the energy from the soul they'd recovered. That was until they got greedy." Matthew gestured to Braun, and both men stood and moved away, whispering in the corner of the interrogation room next to Nash.

Geri's sisters killed Hetty. *But why?* Lila cleared her throat. "Gentlemen?" She rattled her chains again, but the whispering duo ignored her.

Nash surged to his feet and whined; his eyes trained on the door.

Lila grinned and sat back in the chair, ready and waiting for the show to start. Her Harrow rescue posse had arrived.

The door slammed open, creating a dent in the wall. Outlined in the doorway was Elspeth, while Aggie, Braun's mother, lurked close behind. Xandie crowded in behind the older women. "Oh, you boys have some explaining to do."

Braun held his hands up, trying to placate the Harrow matriarch. "Now, Elspeth. Just calm down and think this through."

Aggie covered her face and took a large step away from Elspeth, muttering under her breath about children who don't think their own actions through.

"Calm down?" Elspeth shrieked. "I'll give you calm, traitor bear." She clapped her hands and blue darts of electricity wreathed her fingers. She pointed a sharp nail at Lila's spelled cuffs.

Holding her hands up, Lila winced as a tiny needle of electricity bit into her wrists for a moment before disappearing, along with the cuffs. "Told you so. Elspeth can spot chaos and incarcerated Harrows a mile away."

"Whoever you are, this is a joint police and reaper operation. You need to stand down and we'll deal with you after our interview concludes." Grim adjusted his stance and drew his pen-sized scythe.

"Trust me, reaper. With me, size does matters." Elspeth drew a water balloon out of her hot pink jogging suit and threw it at the reaper's feet.

"See," Lila crowed. "That's what I said. In your face, Grim."

Gray and pink-colored smoke quickly covered the room.

"Time for you to leave, Lila dear." Elspeth cackled and the lights flickered in the interrogation room. A set of red eyes blinked next to the man, visible through the smoke. "Get a move on, puppy. Gotta be quick to keep up with a Harrow.

Nash's red eyes blinked and flickered back to normal as he sauntered past the cursing law enforcement duo. The hellhound paused and raised his leg next to the reaper.

Matthew leapt back as liquid splashed over him

and jagged arcs of electricity from Elspeth's zapping fingers interacted with a sizzle.

Xandie crept into the room. "Come on, cousin. Let's clear out so Braun and his friend can calm down." She snagged Lila's arm as Nash scampered over to Lila and stretched, his mouth wide open in a got-your-back grin. Xandie shoved Lila quickly through the open door.

Braun bellowed. "Alexandra Meyers, don't you dare interfere."

"Sorry, sweetie. Family first." Xandie grimaced and avoided her mother, Miranda, who bent over laughing, tears rolling down her face.

Lila paused in the doorway, enjoying the sight of the big tough bear shifter and grumpy reaper yelping as Elspeth alternated blue and pink jabs of electricity at their tushes.

"You won this round, Lila Harrow. But I'll be watching you," Grim roared and flung his scythe up to block an Elspeth-powered neon pink strike.

"Yeah, but I have the Wolverine of witches, and she's mad." Lila giggled at the sight of the two burly men dodging Elspeth's bolts in a bizarre dance. The smoke dissipated enough that the two men's furious glances were obvious. "See you later, boys." Lila finger waved to Braun and Grim.

"Be seeing you sooner rather than later, *landlord*."

Lila ducked out of the doorway and groaned. She'd forgotten his family business had rented the other apartment. As an ominous warning, his last words were gold.

Lila had a horrible feeling she'd pay double for Elspeth's electric zaps to the tush.

"He did it on purpose. For hours. Bang. Bang. Bang." Lila lowered her head onto her crossed arms and yawned.

"You did set the wicked witch of Point Muse onto him. He probably still has singe marks on his..." Holly pointed to Lila's bottom.

"Hey." Lila jerked her head up and glared. "Not my fault. Incarcerated at the time, remember? Can't control Elspeth from an interrogation room."

"Can't control Elspeth at any time."

Xandie winced at Holly's words and held her hand up. "That may have been my fault. Zach's sister, Melody, rang me when the boys brought you in for questioning. Elspeth overheard and hit the warpath, dragging us along with her."

"Boys? They're years past boys." Lila opened her mouth in a bone-cracking yawn and pushed her wild brown curls out of her face. "Boys don't drive my customers away. Law enforcement does."

"Actually, to be fair, Elspeth does. I call it the Elspeth syndrome. The town's waiting to see what she does to the reaper and since he's lodging upstairs, the bakery is in the possible fallout zone." Holly nodded sagely. "At least Hester's happy."

All three Harrows looked over at the tiny Brownie holding a glossy magazine and giggling.

"I'm kind of freaked out. I've never seen her smile, let alone laugh. It feels wrong." Holly shivered and wrapped her arms around her stomach.

Lila shrugged. "She has an unhealthy love of supernatural gossip mags. With no customers, she can read as many as she likes."

"Where's the new girl, Janie?"

Lila answered Xandie's question by opening the door between the bakery and the kitchen. Janie stood at Lila's scarred island bench, facing them. The bakery assistant stiffened and waved at the Harrow cousins as she whispered something into the phone. Then in a louder voice squealed, "I know. He's so cute, he's a reaper *and* he's living above the bakery."

Lila slammed the door shut. The Grim Reaper

was a hit with everyone but her. "Janie's been glued to the phone since she arrived this morning for work. Apparently, the reaper's a hot topic."

Nash whimpered and settled next to Lila, his muzzle resting on giant paws, staring soulfully up at her.

"Not your fault those nasty lawmen tired you out, so you slept through my interrogation." Lila bit her lip. "But nice touch when you peed on Grim. Who's a good boy?" Lila smothered Nash's head in kisses.

Holly shuddered. "Never ever will I become a pet owner. All those germs from kissing his head. Yuck." She fake-gagged and pointedly moved away from the hound, closer to Xandie.

"Hey, I gave him a bath. Nash is squeaky clean."

"Not him, you. Do you know how many germs the human mouth has? And you just slathered that poor puppy in mouth germs."

"He's the runt offspring of a ferocious hellhound and Cerberus, the three-headed, flame-belching guard dog of hell. I'm pretty sure the puppy will survive."

Theo, Xandie's ancient Greek teenager turned feline guardian to the supernatural Great Library of Alexandria, spat up a fur ball and pushed it toward

Holly. "Here, I saved this for later, but if you need to calm down, it's yours."

Holly gagged, this time for real, and forced out words around her nausea, "Thanks, but I'd never take your regurgitated fur from you. It's all yours."

"I like death girl. She has manners." Theo patted this fur ball over to underneath Hester's table.

"See, never having a pet."

"Mine came with the job. Not a lot of choice." Xandie shrugged. "I'd rather hear about the hot reaper. Couldn't get much of a look through Elspeth's smoke bomb."

Hester slammed her magazine down on the table, surprising a yowl of protest from Theo. "You're all disturbing my reading. So, let's get this out of the way." Hester swiveled and pointed at Lila. "She sneers at the reaper, but secretly thinks he's hot. He thinks she's a murder suspect but can't seem to get her witchy hotness out of his mind. This makes them both crappy and in denial. They will tear metaphorical strips off each other, all the time battling an intense attraction. More dead bodies will follow, they'll be forced to work together and bam... another Harrow hook up." Hester dusted her hands. "Now, can I please get back to the gossip columns?"

Holly stared in awe at the Brownie. "It's like she's an Oracle. Her words ring true."

Lila smacked the back of her cousin's head. "Seriously? She literally just read the premise of the latest Bespelled murder mystery movie. There's one born every minute."

"Doesn't mean she isn't right." Xandie poked her tongue out at her cousin. "Don't forget how Zach and I were when I first arrived in Point Muse. More fight than flirt. But it soon changed."

Lila snorted. "Please, the sparks were flying from the beginning, unlike that reaper and me. Plus, he thinks I'm a killer."

"Hetty died eating one of your cupcakes. It would be a fairly obvious deduction to make," Holly pointed out with a shrug.

A sudden gust of wind on an otherwise calm day blew the bakery door open. Elspeth stood outlined in the doorway before she shoved a small hissing woman inside. "The Harrows ain't going down for murder. Not on my watch." Elspeth dragged the short, plump woman into the center of the room. "Tell them."

The older lady hissed at Elspeth, "This squares us. Got it, Harrow?"

"Yeah, yeah." Elspeth waved a hand. "Spill, mouse."

A gold sheen flickered over the woman's eyes. "I hate it when you call me that."

"Who cares, shapeshifter. Tell them."

The woman huffed. "Fine. I live just down from Hetty's place. The other day I was out weeding my garden—"

Elspeth interrupted with a cough. "You mean sleeping in your garden."

"Do you want me to tell them or not?" The woman glared at the Harrow matriarch.

"Why was she sleeping in the garden?" Xandie whispered.

Lila nodded to the small woman. "She's a shifter, badger, I think. She sleeps in the garden sometimes."

Holly joined the conversation. "So why call her mouse?"

"Because she's a timid poker player. I'm more a seize the day and pot kind of gal," Elspeth said.

"And you cheat," Mouse sneered at her fellow poker player.

Elspeth waved a blue-tipped finger at the shifter. "Carry on, or I'll call in my IOU."

"Argh." Mouse fluffed her dyed brown hair. "From my place I can see the back of Geri' shop and part of the alley. I saw Hetty watching Geri's shop over the fence on her day visit back home. Two women, one older, one younger, argued behind the shop. One of the women left and the other stayed behind." Mouse paused for a breath.

Two women arguing? That could happen on any day—any day and any resident of Point Muse. "And…"

"Geri came out and had words with one of the women, and then headed back inside. The other lady disappeared. A while later someone in a hooded jumper turned up and let themselves in. They were probably in there for a few minutes and then bolted out the back door again. Ten minutes after that, two different women turned up. I heard a commotion from inside the shop, then they bolted too. Well, I say bolted, but they were pretty old and decrepit looking, so more a fast walk. Then I heard the sirens and saw the flashing lights when Braun and the healers turned up soon after that." Mouse turned to Elspeth and glared. "That's all I know. Debt repaid. Got it, Harrow?"

Elspeth rolled her eyes. "Until next time when I wipe the floor in poker with you."

Lila held a hand. "Can I ask you a question?"

"You're a Harrow, no one can stop you talking."

Ignoring the grumpy badger, Lila ploughed on. "You said Hetty was in her garden and saw the whole thing, same as you?"

"Yep, standing at her fence line, pretending to water her plants."

"And Hetty would've been in full view of anyone at the back of Geri's shop?"

"Yes." Mouse tapped her foot.

"That means the killer saw Hetty. It's probably why she was killed. Did they see you?"

Mouse snorted, sounding like the grumpy badger she was. "I burrowed into the ground, only my snout and eyes poked out. There's a gap in my fence just at the right level for peering out at people. No one could have seen me. Now if we're all done, I'm off for a nap." Mouse spun and flounced out of the bakery after a sidelong glare at Elspeth. The door slammed shut behind her.

"Well, that's my good deed for the day." Elspeth dusted off her hands. "Aggie and I have a date with the Internet."

Lila froze, a deer-in-headlights-look upon her face. "You aren't doing any internet shopping are you? We still have fifty backscratchers left from the last time you shopped online."

Elspeth cackled and the lights sizzled overhead

with a pop. "We are shopping...of a kind." She rubbed her hands and let loose a villainous laugh.

Holly closed her eyes, muttering under her breath, "Please, don't let it be me. Please. Please. Please."

Lila rolled her eyes at her cousin's antics. "Calm down, death girl. She's given up on hooking us up with the fairer sex."

"Oh, I have. You're both lost causes and will be old maids with a hundred cats and a body odor problem. No. We're swiping right, or is it left? I forget." Elspeth shrugged, unconcerned. "We're man hunting for Aggie. She has a bear itch that needs scratching."

Xandie shuddered and backed away, fingers in her ears, humming. "I heard nothing. I have no clue what my grandmother and my boyfriend's mother have planned. I. Know. Nothing."

"The backbone of the next generation disappoints me. All pious, lily-livered prudish witches. What a shame." Elspeth tapped her chin. "I might have a potion for that... Tootles." With a malicious smirk, their grandmother disappeared outside.

"I'd check any food or drink you get from that hag for the next few days, if I were you." Hester looked up briefly before dropping her gaze down to her magazine again.

"I'm more concerned about one of my customers being a homicidal maniac. The killer likely took Hetty out because she saw them. Whoever the murderer is, they must have overheard Susie, Hetty's daughter, telling me her mom wanted to talk to me. The killer's watching and following me. That's the only way they could've heard." *Why would any resident of Point Muse want to do away with Hetty? She was harmless, friends with everyone.*

"They didn't need to follow you. They saw Hetty, she was just a witness to remove. Susie talking to you and sending you to the retirement home is just the icing on the cupcake."

Lila let out a breath. "I'd rather the murderer not be one of my customers. Cuts down on my revenue streams if the killer bumps off another regular and then gets arrested."

"That's cold, Lila Marie. Cold." Holly shook her head.

"That's business for you. It's cutthroat." A silver-haired woman in a hot pink business suit took a measured step inside the bakery. "Maybe you should assess whether you're cut out for the baking world.

Nothing to be ashamed about if you can't cope." The woman smiled shark teeth at Lila and her family.

The kitchen door swung open and Janie poked her head out. Her eyes widened when she spotted the other woman and then she quickly dropped out of sight again.

"My business sense has nothing to do with you." Lila crossed her arms and glared. "And who are you anyway?"

The woman trilled and patted her silver hair back into her up-swept hairdo. "My goodness, how silly am I? Marie Hestis from Hestia's Wholesome Healthy Hits. I spoke to you on the phone about your decadent brownie recipe."

Lila snapped her fingers. "The brownie stalker? No offence, Hester."

Hester shrugged and ignored Lila.

"Well, I wouldn't put it quite like that. But Hestia would like to partner with you in a decadent Brownie enterprise." Marie made a face as she glanced around the empty bakery. "Frankly, I think we're doing you a favor. Considering the lack of customers in here, this might be your only chance before your bakery suffers worse setbacks."

"Setbacks?" *Who did this woman think she was?*

"Why, the murders, of course. All connected to

your bakery. It's the hottest news of the baking world. Quite a shame really. Your little shop does have the most delicious nibbles." Marie strolled around the bakery, trailing fingers across the tables.

Why, that... Lila launched herself at the woman, hands outstretched.

Xandie and Holly yanked a fuming Lila back and anchored her between them.

"The murders have nothing to do with me *or* my bakery," she insisted in a very loud voice.

"Of course not, sweetie." Marie tapped the side of her nose. "You know that, and I know that, but the buying public is not quite as clued in as we are. They see the police taking you in for questioning and then..." She snapped her fingers. "They desert you because they think you're a baked goods killer. Sad fact. That's why Hestia's giving you this one last chance." Marie held up one finger. "And you'd be smart to take it."

Lila shook off her cousins' restraining hands and clenched her fingers into tight fists. "Or what?"

"I'd be interested in hearing this *or what?*" Matthew Grim stood in the doorway. A softly growling Nash, eyes flickering red off and on, stood beside him.

"I have no clue who you are, but I'm offering Ms.

Harrow a mutually beneficial business proposition and considering she's a murder suspect, it would be in her best interest to take the deal."

Matthew strolled into the room and leaned against the counter. He scowled at the woman, his beaky nose making his face look more rugged than normal. Lila glared at the reaper and her traitorous puppy as he settled at the reaper's feet.

Matthew dropped his casual stance and growled at the Hestia employee. "Nothing's been said about Lila Marie Harrow being a murder suspect. In fact, I'd be interested to learn where you heard the police were interviewing her?"

Flustered, Marie took a few steps back toward the bakery door. "Just a rumor floating around town. You know how small towns are." She nodded at Lila. "Our offer to buy your recipes, including the brownie recipe, still stands. Here are all my contact details." The rep flicked a business card that landed at Lila's feet. "Don't take too long. I'm only in town for a small amount of time." With that, she spun around and left.

Expelling the breath, she'd been holding, Lila sagged into a chair and flicked a glance at the reaper. "You have a talent for getting rid of rubbish quickly. I'm impressed."

Nash's eyes flickered back to their normal dark brown and he collapsed on Lila's feet.

She lowered her hand and scratched behind his ears.

"It's a gift," Matthew said. "Just like yours is to cause drama. Why the heavy pressure business deal?"

"Hestia's been after my brownie recipe for a while. I guess the rep's taking advantage of the situation to pressure me into selling."

Grim nodded and headed for the door of the bakery. He paused for a moment. "How about you stay away from trouble and let the experts find the killer? Stick to your baking." With that, he let the door slam closed.

Well, heck, he'd left without even telling her why he'd popped into the bakery. Although he had a perfect right. After all, he lived upstairs. And as for his 'stick to baking' comment? Lila knew just where she'd shove her baking all right. Lila Harrow was on the hunt for a killer and the reaper better not get in her way.

Or he'd find out just how nasty a witchy baker could get.

"Scandinavian skipping skunks." Lila bolted out of the kitchen and into the shop, hands clasped over her potty mouth. She slammed the door shut behind her, leaned against it and dragged deep breaths of pure, clean, non-spoiled air into her lungs.

Scrabbling noises sounded on the other side of the door. Lila jerked it open.

Nash stumbled out, whimpering. He huddled in the corner of the bakery, heaving up fluorescent-green hellhound goo.

"Oh no, Nash." Lila bolted over to her distressed hellhound. "I'm so sorry, sweetie. I didn't realize I'd left you behind." She stroked the trembling puppy.

"Kid's got no staying power." Colin, Elspeth's annoying pug, strutted into the bakery with Holly by his side. "I, on the other hand, am a master of clearing a room and not heaving."

Lila glared at the walking, farting, talking offence against Mother Nature. "It's not his fault. Somehow the fridge was left open overnight. Everything spoiled, it's an olfactory assault on the senses and he's just a puppy with a keen sniffer."

Nash leaned against Lila's leg and huffed a hell-hound version of laughter at the pug.

Colin's eyes narrowed. "Don't think I don't know what you're doing, hell-beast. But you'll lose. The Harrows were mine first."

Holly took a prudent step away from Colin's fallout zone just in case he happened to let loose with a punishing blast of pug flatulence. "The Harrows belong to no one. Nash's dad is a hellhound and his mother's the three-headed dog who guards hell. I wouldn't upset him either."

"Whatever, doll face." Colin strutted past Nash and lifted his leg only to drop it when Lila made cutting motions. "This ain't over, hellhound." Sticking his nose in the air, he trotted over to a small couch set close to the old-fashioned fireplace and hauled himself up.

Holly strolled toward the kitchen door. "Male dominance rearing its ugly head. Colin has been like that since your mom gave you Nash. He's trying to exert control over the situation."

Lila held a hand up. "Holly? I wouldn't do that if I was you."

Pushing open the door to the kitchen, Holly took a step in. "I deal with dead bodies. I'm pretty sure I can cope with whatever the fridge drama is." The door slammed shut behind her.

Lila crept toward the kitchen and listened against the door but heard nothing but a strange gurgling noise. "Holly? You okay?" She waited for a moment before trying again. "Death girl? Can you hear me? Knock once for yes. Do you need assistance? I repeat, do you need assistance?" She yelled the last word and banged on the door.

"Is this normal for Point Muse?"

Matthew Grim's low, gravelly voice raked over Lila's nerve endings as his breath tickled her nape. Screeching, she turned around and slapped the reaper's chest. "Can't you get a bell around your neck or something? You almost scared the Harrow out of me."

"I don't think it's possible to lose your Harrowness." He twitched an eyebrow at Lila's hand, still lying flat on his chest.

"Whoops" Lila moved her hand away from

Matthew's solid muscled chest that she refused to take notice of. The gurgling noise grew louder from behind the kitchen door. *Holly.* Lila spun back to the door. "Can you hear me?"

"Is there a problem with your door that you can't open it and see if your cousin requires help?"

"Yes, there's a problem. If we open the door, we risk letting lethal gases out of the kitchen." Sarcasm coated Lila's words, forcing back the memory of reaper muscle.

"Okay. Maybe I can help you then." Grim slipped his hands around Lila's waist, lifted her and placed her a few steps away from the door.

"I wouldn't do that if I was you. I tried to warn Holly, but she ignored me," Lila pointed out helpfully.

"You said there's gas in the kitchen and your cousin's inside. Someone has to help her."

Colin snorted from the direction of the couch. "That's the way these Harrows are. Suck you in until your part of the family. Then abandon you when someone younger turns up. They're poison, man. Poison."

"Zip it, Colin." Lila threw a dishtowel at the mouthy pug, then grabbed another and shoved it at

Grim. "If you want to be a hero it's up to you. But at least protect your senses."

Grim wrapped the dishtowel around his head, covering his mouth and nose.

"May the hex protect you." Lila lowered her head, honoring the reaper's sacrifice. A snicker escaped her tight control.

Matthew grunted and opened the door, sliding into the kitchen.

An unmanly shriek, followed by a high-pitched gurgling, filtered through the kitchen door.

"You need to give the guy a break, toots. He honestly thinks he's rescuing the Banshee from toxic gases and you're a callous cousin for not being more worried."

"Seriously, Colin? I liked you better when you couldn't talk and just humped everything that moved." Lila ignored Colin's affronted protests. But the mouthy dog had a point. Matthew had no clue what he was about to take on, but still he charged in, ready to rescue the Banshee in distress even if it was only by a toxic fridge leak.

The kitchen door swung open, slammed Lila on the forehead and sent her flying to the ground. She groaned and rolled over, lying flat on her back.

Grim carried Holly over his shoulder in a fireman's lift.

Holly raised a fluttering hand off her rescuer's back. "You left me behind. Left me to expire. Death by toxic fridge sludge is not the way I want to go out."

Lila pushed herself to a sitting position and winced as she pressed on the growing lump on her forehead. "I told you to stop. *But no.* You're a banshee used to death. *You can handle anything.* It's all your own fault."

Matthew dumped Holly onto a chair close to the pug. "An open fridge door is not an emergency or a toxic gas leak." He rubbed the left side of his neck.

Holly sat up, scowling. "For your information, someone attached a hex to the fridge. Made everything spoil and rot, so it could have ended up as toxic gas. It could yet be deadly."

"Who would hex my fridge? I mean, it's smelly and inconvenient, but I can still just go to the store and pick up replacement ingredients. Why bother?" Lila stood and stretched her back out, stopping when she felt the reaper's eyes on her. Heat spread from Lila's stomach and flushed upward.

Holly frowned, then with eyes wide, pointed at Lila. "You blushed. What's wrong? Are you sick?

Has the toxic gas leak affected your internal heat regulation?"

Colin snickered in the background and even Nash burbled mockingly.

"Can we focus on the fact that someone sabotaged my produce?" Lila pointed at Matthew, ignoring his wide shoulders and the beaky nose that had become increasingly attractive. "If someone's targeting me, that means I can't be a murder suspect."

"A murder suspect can still have multiple enemies. Who knows how many people you've upset in Point Muse? Doesn't cross you off as a suspect."

"Hey, not fair. You told the pushy Hestia rep I wasn't a suspect," Lila objected.

"I lie. It's a reaper thing. Besides, if you aren't the killer, you still might lead me to them. I've heard about the Harrow luck in finding dead bodies." Grim strolled through the doorway leading to upstairs.

"That's my cousin Xandie's gift, finding bodies, and she's Meyers, not a Harrow," Lila hollered back.

"Great comeback. I think he likes you." Holly nodded sagely. "He has that vibe."

Lila thrust her hands up in the air. "There's no vibe. None. No vibrations. Only mutual loathing."

"Methinks the baker witch protests too much."

"Zip it, Colin," both Harrows shouted at the pug.

"Fine. I'm leaving. There's no love in this bakery. My Elspeth will hear about your meanness and lack of snack offerings." Colin jumped from the couch and strutted past Nash, pausing only to glare at the puppy until Nash whimpered and placed paws over his eyes. "That's right, puppy. I'm the boss." Sniffing, Colin stomped to the bakery door and scooted through it when Janie held it wide.

The assistant paused uncertainly when she spotted the two Harrow cousins staring at her. "I was supposed to work today, right?"

"Sorry. We just had a minor toxic spell. Holly was saved, so it's all good."

"Right." Looking confused, Janie shut the door. "Do you still want me to unload the delivery? The truck has normally dropped our order in the alley by now."

In the drama of the toxic fridge, she'd forgotten all about her impending delivery. "Sorry, I have no clue if he's even done the delivery yet. We had a fridge issue, and trust me, you don't want to go into the kitchen yet." Lila shuddered.

"Actually, the reaper countered the hex with vinegar and opened the window," Holly said. "The toxic smell is all gone, you just need to clean out the fridge sludge."

"Right. Janie, you're on fridge cleanup duty and I'll chase up the delivery." Lila grabbed Janie's hand and dragged her assistant into the kitchen, directing her to the fridge. "I'll be in the alley, waiting for the delivery. Crack on, bakery minion." Lila skipped into the alley. "It's good to be boss." She rubbed at a tacky black smear that decorated her palm. "Where did that come from?" Lila wiped the mark on her jeans and leaned against the brick wall, tapping her fingers as she waited. She checked her watch as the minutes ticked over. "Ralph is late." Frowning, Lila walked to the mouth of the alley and peered along Main Street. Ralph, obsessive timekeeper, would never be late.

"Miss Lila." The baldheaded, skinny as a rake, delivery driver, rushed up. "I'm so sorry. The truck's broken down and we still have three deliveries to make, including yours."

Another issue but at least this one wasn't sabotage. "No worries, Ralph. You can't help it if your truck breaks down." Lila patted the anxious man on the shoulder.

"That's the thing, the old girl was running fine, then I popped into the grocery store to grab another order. Then, bam. Nothing works. She only had a service yesterday. I don't get it." Ralph wrung his hands.

Then again, maybe it was sabotage? "The garage still services your truck?"

Ralph nodded.

"Do me a favor and get Aaron to check it out. See if anything foreign caused the breakdown."

"Foreign?"

"Hex related."

Ralph stepped back. "I ain't messing with Elspeth Harrow. She got no reason to hex me or my truck."

Lila rolled her eyes. "We live in a magical town founded on leylines, populated by magical creatures. More than one person in Point Muse knows how to hex."

"Gotcha." Ralph rubbed his bald head. "Aaron will give us a run-around truck to use as a replacement. We'll get your delivery out as soon as we can."

Lila nodded and winked at the truck driver. "Be wary of strangers carrying hexes."

Grunting his thanks, Ralph hurried off.

She'd bet her last cupcake someone hexed the delivery truck. *But why?* Just to get back at Lila? Or to distract her from the murders and her hunt for the killer? Lila pushed open the alley door and surprised Janie on the phone again.

"It's done, okay. Now leave me alone," Janie hissed into the phone and hung up abruptly when she spotted Lila. She pointed at the fridge. "Do I get danger pay cleaning the fridge?"

Poor little Janie, having a relationship crisis on the phone. True love, always a bumpy road. Deciding to give her assistant a break, Lila winked. "No pay rise, but if you want a little extra time for lunch to deal with that," Lila pointed to Janie's phone. "Go for it."

"Sorry?"

"Whatever relationship drama you're dealing with. Take extra time at lunch to fix it. Not all of us want to be old maids."

"Oh. Right. Thanks." Janie forced a laugh. "Sorry. I know I'm not supposed to get phone calls at work."

Lila waved Janie's words away. "Don't stress, but if you can clean that fridge, I'll be grateful. Thankfully, we're opening late today." Nodding to Janie, Lila headed out the front. She stood next to the counter and gestured to her cousin.

Sighing, Holly dragged herself from the chair. "What now, oh bakery Queen?"

Lila lowered her voice. "I think someone's trying to distract me from finding the killer."

"Why are we whispering?"

"Because I don't want that freeloader upstairs to hear me."

"He poked his head in here before to let me know he might be heading out. No need to whisper."

"Oh." Lila raised her voice to normal Harrow levels. "Anyway, I spoke to Ralph. My delivery truck driver. His van broke down and Aaron only serviced it yesterday. I'm betting someone hexed the truck just like my fridge."

"Great, someone after Harrow blood again. Really, I don't know what we do to deserve this type of nastiness constantly."

"Some kind of Elspeth-related drama? Karma, probably." Lila bit her lip. "You said Grim headed out? Did he say where he was going?"

"Nope." Holly shrugged and then pointed at her chest. "Banshee, not the keeper of Grim's diary, remember?"

"Fine." She'd hunt the killer on her own. First step, finding out where Matthew had gone. "Keep a lookout for me."

"Why am I giving you free labor?"

"Because I'm taking a page out of Xandie's sleuthing book and I'm searching Grim's apartment."

"Your funeral." Holly waved her cousin off.

Lila crept up the stairs toward her and the reaper's apartments. Holly's words echoed ominously in her ears.

With the way her luck was shaping up, it might just be her one-way ticket to Hell if Grim caught her...

NINE

"If he didn't want me to sneak in, why is his door unlocked? As far as I'm concerned that's an open invitation. Right?" Lila glanced at a grumbling Nash at her feet. "Hey, you're supposed to be my minion. No whining or negative comments aloud."

Nash took a step over the apartment threshold then immediately curled up on the floor.

"Everyone's a critic." Wrinkling her nose, Lila wandered around the carbon copy of her own apartment. "Elspeth must have got a discount if she bought everything in multiples." Truthfully, Lila called the building that housed her apartment and the bakery hers. But Elspeth paid the bills and obviously controlled who rented out the spare apartment.

"My place is much better. Grim must like sterile." Lila frowned.

Not an ounce of color. No personal touch, no photos or even a stray teddy bear lined the room. "Dude, you need to Elspeth up your life." Her grandmother drove her crazy, but life wasn't dull.

"Seriously, Nash. Give a witch a hand here?"

Nash rolled onto his back and cycled his paws in the air.

"Everyone's a comedian. Big, bad hellhound. So scary." Lila rolled her eyes. "If I was a suspicious reaper, with no imagination, where would I hide my secret information from the nosy baker?" Lila dropped to her knees next to a truly ugly coffee table in the shape of a witch's hat and slid her hand underneath. "Bingo." She gripped the manila folder and drew it out. "This sleuthing gig is kind of easy."

Lila opened the folder and flicked through the contents. "Background information on Point Muse, its residents and threat levels." Lila snorted. *What were the odds the Harrows featured heavily in the paperwork?* Interested, she scanned the page. "Wow, Elspeth. Rocking the wicked witch label." Her grandmother had a list of cautions, warnings and arrests that carried over onto the next page. Even her own mother, Amelia, had a paragraph of cautions and arrests for protesting animal cruelty. The only thing her Aunt Winifred had was a caution for inhaling witchy herbs in a public place. "No wonder Harrows have a reputation in town," Lila grumbled.

She carried on flicking through the folder. "Oh, no, you didn't, Grim." A handful of black-and-white photos slid into her hand. Hissing, Lila fumed. "That's an invasion of privacy. Nash, do you see that?" Lila flapped a photo in the air at the now snoring puppy. "That's my bakery. He's taken photos of my bakery, my apartment. Even when I stepped out into the alley to put the garbage cans out." She moaned. "Why did I wear my fuzzy unicorn slippers and why didn't I at least comb my hair? I look like Frankenstein's bride with a unicorn fetish."

Nash rolled over and opened one eye, his snoring sounding suspiciously like a snicker. Lila waggled a finger at her puppy. "You better not be making fun of me, hound. Otherwise, I'll tell mother it's time for a certain snip-snip surgery."

Nash closed his eyes and pretended to doggy snore.

"That's what I thought." Winking at her sleep-faking puppy, Lila continued through the folder. She plucked a formal looking document from amongst the surveillance photos and read it aloud. "Threat level for Lila Marie Harrow is low to average. Her ability to incite emotion in those who sample her food has chaos possibilities, but the effect has a limited timeframe. Other family members have higher threat levels."

She blew a raspberry at the report. "I could be a threat if I wanted. I just like to bake. I could probably make my witchy gifts affect my customers for longer. But I'm about good vibes, not Elspeth wickedness." What do those judgy reapers know, anyway?

All she found out so far was that Grim had been watching the Harrows and her bakery for a while. She needed to know about the victims and the hag sisters instead of how she wore her unicorn slippers. Growling, Lila threw the folder on the coffee table. The papers slid out and one page caught Lila's attention.

"Autopsy report for Geri Keres and Henrietta Barnes." Lila took a deep breath, girding her baking loins. She wasn't death obsessed like Holly. This type of thing scared the sugar from her soul. But if she wanted to find the killer, she had no choice. Lila picked the piece of paper up and scanned it. The local healer at Point Muse hospital had overseen the autopsy of both women.

"The first victim had a contusion on the back of the skull that cracked the bone. This caused traumatic brain injury and a brain hemorrhage. The victim died shortly after the initial injury. The second victim, Henrietta Barnes, had injuries consistent with choking on a cupcake, causing throat irritation, as well as throat damage and death by asphyxiation. But bruising was noted on cheeks and face as if held down. A small cross incision noted on the palm of the hand."

Lila slapped the page onto the coffee table. "Now I feel like a very sweet hot chocolate. I am channeling Xandie. Poor Hetty. Death by her favorite Vanilla Viagra for the Soul cupcake." She shuddered. Not the way that Lila would want to go out. Something was niggling at her about the way Geri had died. "If Geri was the third soul-sucking death demon, how could you possibly die by head trauma? Wasn't she immortal?"

Nash leapt up and plodded to the door of the apartment, pawing at the wood.

"You're right, sweetie. We need to get out of here before that nosy man springs us." Lila gathered the papers into the folder and stuck it back under the coffee table.

"You can't hide anything from Lila Harrow. Point Muse's number two sleuth." Snickering, Lila headed for the door and slipped out into the hallway.

"Cuckoo. Cuckoo," Holly trilled up the stairs.

"What are you? A German clock?" The funeral home had addled her cousin's brain.

The slam of the door downstairs and Holly's overly loud greeting froze Lila momentarily.

"Matthew. You weren't gone long. Can I interest you in a *hide-now* cupcake?"

"Interesting choice of food naming."

Hecate's toenails. Grim! Lila shoved Nash back inside the apartment, shutting the door and locking it.

"Part of Lila's charms are her strange naming skills. My favorite is the Death by Chocolate Brownies." Holly paused for a moment and awkward silence spread. "Not that her brownies have actually killed anyone. They just make you feel a little naughty," she hurriedly added.

"I think I'll pass. If you'll excuse me."

A muffled thump sounded from downstairs. Lila rolled her eyes. Holly probably tried to bodily waylay the reaper. Considering the size difference, it was next to useless. Lila spun to face the apartment door as Grim cleared the top of the stairs. She thumped on the wood. "Nash, can you hear me, sweetie? Did my little man get stuck in that nasty reaper's apartment?"

"Tried to get into my apartment, did you, little witch?" Matthew crossed arms over a solid chest and his eyebrows beetled over narrowed gray eyes.

"I would never search your personal space. But Nash is missing, and I think he's in your apartment." Indignation swept through Lila's voice. Really, what was he accusing her of? Okay, she had broken in and searched the room, but he didn't know that. Besides, Elspeth would hex her if she got caught breaking and entering...*again*.

Nash took that moment to whimper behind the door.

Grim's face softened, and he unlocked the door. "Sorry. I just thought..."

Lila sniffed. "You thought because I'm a Harrow that I play loose as an Elspeth goose with the law? Baker, buddy, and don't you forget it."

The reaper opened the door and Nash jumped out, panting. He headed straight to Lila's arms.

"My poor baby. My poor little hellhound." Lila gathered the puppy in for a tight hug.

Matthew took a step into his apartment and

scanned the surroundings. "I don't know how he got in there. He wasn't there when I left. I'm sure of it."

"He's a hellhound and his mother's Cerberus. Who knows what skills he has? I did see him sniffing outside your door earlier. Maybe he thinks you smell good?" Lila made a show of inhaling. Okay, he did kind of smell like cinnamon. One of her favorite spices.

Grim stepped back and winced as his foot slid on a puddle and he grabbed the doorjamb to stay upright.

Both Lila and Grim's gaze slid down to the floor.

She winced and Nash hid his head under Lila's arm. "He must've needed to go out when he got stuck in your place. Sorry about that." She flashed an insincere smile.

Growling, Grim shook his foot and took a large step away. A faint hint of wispy steam lifted off the puddle of hellhound wee.

"Sorry again. I'll leave you to your cleaning. Thanks for letting Nash out," Lila chortled and scampered downstairs.

Holly grabbed Lila as soon as she appeared in the bakery. "What happened? Did he catch you? What did you find out?"

Lila carefully placed Nash on the ground. She

gave him a congratulatory stroke. "You have perfect timing, hound. Remind me to bring you along on all our Harrow breaking and entering jaunts."

"Well?"

"I pretended Nash had been locked inside the apartment. Nash distracted him by peeing on the floor and Grim stepped in it when he let him loose. It was perfect."

Holly sagged against the counter. "Thank Hecate. I thought he'd sprung you for sure. Did you find anything?"

"A file hidden under a table."

"That's a pathetic place to hide something. Elspeth would hex us if we hid our secrets like that."

"He wasn't raised by a wicked Harrow witch; we have to accept his limitations and profit from them." Lila glanced up the stairs and made a prudent decision to close the connecting bakery door. "The reaper has a bunch of information on all the Harrows, including all of our threat levels. I'm low to average. Can you believe that?" Lila wrinkled her nose. She definitely needed to up her threat level. She didn't want Elspeth and Xandie to be the only ones capable of mass mayhem. She had a family reputation to uphold.

"Fancy that," Holly replied dryly. "Anything on the murders?"

"Geri died of a brain hemorrhage and poor Hetty. Not only did she choke on the cupcake that someone shoved down her throat, she also had bruising, plus a cross cut into her palm."

"That may have been the dagger. Did Geri have a cut as well?"

"No. But my question is, if she's a death Daimon, how did someone kill her?"

"We need Xandie and the library."

Lila nodded at her cousin. "You're right. I'll call Hester to take over the bakery. We need answers."

She needed to find the killer pronto before her bakery reputation crumbled completely.

"I can't believe you got poor Nash to pee on him." Xandie raised a hand, and a gold scroll flew into it. She pushed it up onto a shelf.

"Nash peed on the floor. His plan, not mine. All hellhound," Lila protested. But it had come in handy in distracting the suspicious reaper. "We decided we needed the Library's help after that." She settled back into a comfortable leather chair.

Every surface in the Library gleamed. Every shelf, desk, and chair, clean and ready for use. The tables and chairs dotted around the room invited an inquisitive body to sit a while. Ornate wooden shelving filled the room, but what drew Lila's attention were the massive floor-to-ceiling lead-light windows that opened out onto the Library's formal gardens and the cliff with steps down to Xandie's private beach. Lila closed her eyes, breathed deep, and soaked up the bookish atmosphere.

"Are you going to sleep?" Xandie accused her cousin in a shrill tone, her hands on her hips.

The lights overhead dimmed for sleeping comfort.

Lila opened one eye. "I'm absorbing the Library's calming vibes. Don't harsh my buzz."

"I'd have thought murder would crush any buzz symptoms you were experiencing." Theo, Xandie's black cat guardian, glared down at Lila from a perch on a shelf above her head.

Warily, Lila opened both eyes. Theo had a temper and claws to match. One tended to forget he'd been an ancient Greek teenager obsessed with mead and ancient scroll porn before the supernatural Great Library of Alexandria had turned him into

Xandie's feline guardian. "What's ruffled your fur, Theo?"

Theo hissed and jerked his whiskers at Lila's feet. "That hellish animal you have desecrated my domicile with."

"Whoa, big words, feline." Lila shrugged. "Can't help it if your pet has a thing for hellhounds."

Everyone stared at Lila's feet where a playful Nash had his tummy rubbed by Theo's enthusiastic imp, Horatio. The little demonic pet wore his flashy hot-pink, Elspeth-bedazzled jogging suit and wide grin as he collapsed against the puppy.

"That mutt has stolen my imp's affections. Probably some nefarious underworld spell." Theo sniffed and stalked toward the puppy, hissing in disgust as Horatio lolled against the hound with a dreamy smile. The cat raised his paw and whacked Nash on the nose, stealing Horatio back.

Nash reared back and his eyes flickered red, smoke trickled out of one nostril.

"Whoops." Xandie scooted and lifted Theo and Horatio out of Nash's reach. "Sorry about that. We talked about your jealous streak, Theo. Nash probably smells familiar to Horatio, the imp and the hellhound are both from the underworld. Horatio has enough love to go around. Share."

Theo grumbled as Xandie pushed the cat and his imp out the library door. "I want it all. Do you hear me? The imp's love and adoration are *all* mine. Mwahaha." The door slammed closed behind Theo's maniacal declarations.

"So, that megalomaniac condition isn't getting any better then?" Lila arched an eyebrow to her shamefaced cousin.

Xandie cleared her throat. "Theo's a work in progress. One that's taking hundreds of years. Now, where were we?"

Holly held up a hand and shifted in her seat like someone with ants in their pants. "Me. I know. The Keres Daimons, Grim Inc and why Geri's dead since she's supposed to be an immortal spirit." She beamed at the room.

"I like it better when you're morose and obsessed with death visions. This perky phase discombobulates me."

Holly poked her tongue out at Lila. "Did you read a big girl dictionary while you were desperate and dateless last night...unlike me." Holly blew on her nails and rubbed them on her jeans.

"With a mortuary assistant." Lila jumped to her feet and paced in front of her Banshee cousin. "Not even the head dead dude. Just an assistant.

Plus, he smells like embalming fluid and has a comb-over."

"The comb-over is genetic. He can't help that. Edwin is a very nice man." Holly glared at her.

"Who drinks embalming fluid? Even Harrows have standards."

"Why, you…" Holly launched herself at Lila with hands outstretched, mimicking her cousin's dramatic style.

Without warning, a heavy leather-bound tome flew through the air. Directed by the Library, it almost knocked the warring cousins out.

"Whoa." Lila reached out and snagged the book. She read the title aloud, "Characteristics of a Death Daimon. Thanks, Library." Lila cleared her throat. "Sorry about the squabbling." With a sniff in Holly's direction, Lila sank into a chair and flicked through the book.

"I have some more information on the reapers as well, but it isn't much." Xandie ignored her cousins as the Library settled back down.

"This is why you're my favorite cousin, Xandie." Holly sat back and waved a hand like a queen to her subject.

"The breakdown is that Matthew Grim's legit. His family has worked as reapers for centuries. The clan has offices all over the world in supernatural hotspots. They work for the greater powers and send souls up and down." Xandie pointed to the ceiling and then to the floor.

Lila chewed. "Why is he here?"

"I guess a murdered body not having a soul is a big no-no in his business." Holly leaned toward her cousin, their temper spat forgotten.

"The scythe they carry is what sucks out the souls and transports them to where they have to go. His family is supposed to be incorruptible. Both Heaven and Hell trust them, so a soul disappearing wouldn't look good. And Zach likes Matthew, they've worked together before. The Grim family are the good guys."

Lila flicked through the Library's book on Demons. "Well, if Zach likes him, then of course, Grim must be okay." Lila's words trailed away as she re-read a page again.

"What?" Holly demanded. "What have you found? You have that look on your face."

"The reason why Geri died of a broken skull instead of being an immortal death demon."

"Care to share with those of us ignorant kids in the rest of the class?" Xandie leaned against the heavy wooden desk.

"It says here that the Keres Daimons are a trio of sisters drawn to bloodied and violent death. They feast on blood-soaked warriors and remove the souls with the Dagger of Degmon. Then they chant the release word in ancient Greek and the souls fly home to Hades. They keep a small portion of the soul's energy as fuel. The rest goes back to Hades."

"And? How does it explain Geri dying?"

"Dad said the trio had rebelled and were eating all of the souls, keeping themselves young instead of sending the souls to Hades. Geri turned on her sisters and then Hades placed her in witness protection. No better place to hide than as a human on a planet populated by them."

"Oh." Xandie nodded. "She may have tattled on her sisters and had to hide from them, but she also still had to be punished, as well. Hades must have stripped her of immortality, making her human."

"Yep. No wonder she liked my Vanilla Viagra for the Soul cupcakes. She needed the energy lift."

"That's so harsh. Made her human and then her sisters killed her." Holly's voice trembled and she bit her lip.

"She might have a human body, but her spirit was all death Daimon. Don't worry, sooky banshee.

We'll catch her sisters and then they'll go back to their Underworld prison."

Lila slammed the book closed and thanked the Library for its help. She wished finding the Keres sisters and handing them back to Hades could be just as easy.

Because for some reason, she had a feeling a showdown in little Point Muse was on the horizon.

TEN

"Three days. That's all I had. Three days of peace and quiet, with no chaos." Lila confronted both Elspeth and Colin, accompanied by the Paladin, Buchanan, outside the bakery.

"Moi?" Elspeth jabbed herself in her bony chest. "I didn't make you stay overnight at Harrow House. That was all your doing."

Malcolm Buchanan, grizzled Paladin and Elspeth's sometimes main squeeze, eyed the Harrow matriarch. "In defense of Lila, you did provide those neon flashing drinks with their own little umbrellas. How's a Harrow woman supposed to resist? Mind you, she didn't need to tabletop can-can with one of your wigs. That was all her."

"Way to stab me in the back, Paladin." Lila

winced as lightning shot through her skull. But he had a point. *Those small baby drinks had been so cute, so tasty and so evil.* "Sorry about the wig thing, Elspeth." Elspeth Harrow lived and died by her wigs. The trashier the better. No one in or out of the family, with the exception of Buchanan and possibly Colin, Elspeth's pug, had even seen her grandmother's real hair.

"Thank you, dear. You will be." Elspeth smirked, shark teeth on show.

"Will be what?"

"Sorry."

Elspeth's words hung in the air. Both Lila and Buchanan, along with Nash, backed away from the wicked witch of Point Muse.

"You know, I kinda liked the wig dancing." Colin panted and twisted his body to gnaw at a spot on his side before giving up. "Lila gets that wacky, fun-loving side from my girl." He rubbed his head on Elspeth's neon green, jogging suit-covered leg.

"Such a sweet thing to say." Elspeth heaved Colin up onto her hip and smothered him in noisy kisses.

He winked at Lila. Great, now she owed the mouthy, food-obsessed pug a favor for distracting Elspeth. She'd be baking for a week. "You didn't turn off my alarm, so I'd turn up late to open the bakery as revenge?"

"I didn't say that." Elspeth winked at Lila and started to walk off before she paused for a moment. "But I definitely didn't turn off your electricity. Tootles."

"Electricity?" Lila questioned Buchanan with wide eyes.

He shrugged. "I have no clue what she means. Sometimes it's best to live the life of the ignorant. That way I have complete deniability when the mayhem hits." He waved at Lila and headed off in the opposite direction to Elspeth.

"Those two get more twisted the more time they spend together." Lila opened the front door of the bakery.

"We have a problem." Hester the Brownie glared at Lila.

"I didn't do it. Whatever's happened, it's not my fault," Lila replied automatically before glancing around the bakery. She spied Janie huddled next to the counter. "What's happened now?"

"You forgot to pay your electricity account. They turned off our power this morning."

"No way, Hester. I never forget to pay my utilities." Lila shook her head in denial. This wasn't her. She knew she'd paid the account.

Janie stepped out from behind the counter. "They rang the shop to inform us they were switching our power off. The account was overdue, and they had no choice and they'd sent out reminder notices. Apparently, they only ring as a last resort. It's a safety measure thing. Seems they'd hoped to catch the owner here when they rang."

"Which I wasn't, courtesy of Elspeth's wig revenge." Lila rubbed her forehead. "Hester, grab the last-minute, go-to stock and go find Aunt Winifred. See if you can get her to defrost everything. Janie, start making multiple batches of icing. Once everything is defrosted, ice the witch out of those cakes. I'll ring the utility company. Now scoot, everyone." Lila clapped her hands and her bakery minions disbursed.

"Nice show of acting under pressure. I'm impressed." Grim leaned against the door to the stairs.

"You still here? There's been no fresh bodies for three days. Doesn't that mean you have to leave now?"

Nash trotted across the room and rubbed against the reaper.

"Traitor." Lila glared at a hellhound puppy.

"Don't blame him. We bonded over a puddle of smoking hellhound urine. We're best buds now. And for your information, I'm here to track the Keres Daimons down. What's happened now?"

"No power. Apparently, the company thinks I'm a nonpaying deadbeat baker."

Matthew frowned. "That's not you. Loud-mouthed, yes. Drama queen, absolutely. Skipping paying a bill so your power gets turned off? No way." The reaper pulled out his phone and made a call. "Ray? Do me a favor and call Point Muse Utilities. Lila Harrow's power is off because she supposedly missed a bill. Sounds fishy. Fix it for me." He hung the phone up. "This isn't the first issue in the last few weeks, is it?"

Lila shrugged. "Harrows are magnets for bad luck, bad romance and dead bodies."

"But?"

"But the last few weeks everything that could go wrong has gone wrong. At least that Hestia woman seems to have disappeared."

Grim nodded but his expression was suspicious. "Is that a good thing or a bad thing? Her disappearance. I mean."

"You know that old saying, keep your friends close and your enemies in the kitchen baking?"

"Close enough." He held up a finger as his phone rang. "What do you have for me, Ray?" Grim grunted and turned his gaze on Lila. "Thanks." The reaper stowed his phone in his pocket just as the lights flickered on.

"Wahoo." Lila threw herself at the shocked man. He caught her mid leap, his arms around her. Lila hugged him and slapped his massive shoulders. "You did it. You might be a know-it-all reaper, but you saved my bakery. Right now, you rock." Lila thumped him on the shoulder again. *Man, the Grim clan built their boys on the large size.* Hard muscle burned her hand and she tapped the still quiet man on his chin. "You can put me down now, big boy."

Matthew cleared his throat and carefully deposited Lila on the floor. "Interesting way of saying thank you."

"They don't call me Drama Llama Lila for nothing. But I really am grateful. Did your friend find the problem?"

"That's the interesting bit. Someone claiming to be you, with all your identity requirements and passwords, called yesterday and cancelled the account. Power to be shut off as of this morning."

"I swear I did not close my account. That's financial suicide for me." Lila sagged into a chair and rested her head on her hand. "Someone really has it in for me and my business."

"I think you're right, and whoever it is, knows you and has access to your paperwork."

Lila jumped up. "Janie said they contacted her just before turning off the power. She's the one who told me my account hadn't been paid."

"Ah... I... I must've got it wrong. I swear that's what I thought they said." Janie stood framed in the kitchen doorway, a bowl of icing in hand. A tear slowly tracked its way down the side of her face. "I wasn't eavesdropping. I just wanted to tell you the power's on again. I must have misunderstood the call. Honestly, it was a mistake. I've had my power turned off before because I missed a bill. I guess I just assumed."

"That's okay, Janie. We have our power back now and nothing had time to spoil. Hester will be back any second. We'll get the food out and everything will be okay."

"I'll get back to the icing." Janie smiled weakly and disappeared back into the kitchen.

A slam of the door and Hester's voice from the kitchen had Lila smiling gratefully. The Brownie would handle Janie and the food. Everything had worked out. *For now*.

"How much do you know about Janie?"

"She likes to eavesdrop and spends too much time on her phone. Not to mention, she's a mess in the kitchen. Pretty much a normal kid in Point Muse."

"Janie isn't a kid, though. And she isn't from Point Muse. She had access to your kitchen and account paperwork," Grim pointed out.

"No offence to Janie, but she's not the sharpest measuring cup in the kitchen. Trust me, it's not her. Maybe those Daimon hags have branched out into the bakery sabotage business?"

"Somehow I doubt ancient Greek death goddesses know how to cancel utility accounts. Just be wary." He checked his watch.

"Hot date, Grim?" He might drive her crazy, but he *was* kind of datable with his floppy dark hair, gray eyes and beaky nose.

"Unless you call a meeting with your father so you can update him on a murder case a hot date."

Lila coughed. "Nope. You're safe. Enjoy your time with your dad."

"I'm briefing my father in person. There's no

enjoy in that scenario. Be careful, Lila." With a nod, the reaper left.

Exhaling, Lila closed her eyes for a moment, enjoying the peace and quiet for once.

"Late to open and sleeping on the job? Not a good start, Ms. Harrow."

Lila opened her eyes and groaned as she realized who'd spoken. "Morning, Clifford. You're in early today."

"It's *Mr. Adams* to you and yours. This is purely business. I have a slot open and decided your Decadent Death by Brownie would be a perfect fill-in."

Good grief. Of all mornings, the food critic for the Point Muse Chronicles had to pick today to review her food. "Of course, *Mr.* Adams. Pick a table and I'll bring a slice of my brownie out for you." Lila watched as he selected a table. Two middle-aged women joined him moments after he sat, despite there being spare tables. She waited for him to send them on their way, but it didn't happen. Then she shrugged and hotfooted it back into the kitchen. Carefully closing the door behind her, Lila banged her head a few times on the wood for emphasis. Clifford Adams was a tight-necked whiner of epic proportions. Elspeth hexed on principle as soon as she saw him. She never could stand whining in a kid or adult.

"What other disaster do we have brewing now?" Hester scowled.

"Clifford Adams is here professionally. He wants to try our famous brownie."

Hester's sharp intake of breath echoed loudly in the quiet kitchen. The little Brownie snapped into action. She pointed at Janie. "Get that icing ready. Lila can plate up and I'll get his soy mocha latte ready."

Lila quickly covered the brownie with the icing Janie had already prepared. A quick wipe of the plate, a sprinkle of icing sugar and a sprig of mint completed her artwork. "Hester, please deliver Adams his brownie. Janie, man the counter and I'll get the rest of the stock ready to go." Leaning against the door after Hester marched out, Lila sighed. Clifford Adams was one of the most snooty, annoying men she'd ever encountered. Unfortunately, whenever he reviewed her food, she definitely saw an increase in customers. And with the last two murder victims both having cupcakes on hand when they died, she needed all the good publicity she could get.

The door opened behind Lila, shoving her forward a step.

Janie poked her head out. "We're filling up quickly. Hester said to get your butt into gear and get the food out to fill up our display cases."

Forcing a smile, Lila waved Janie off and grabbed the trays, carefully placing her prepared food onto them before heading out front.

Janie grabbed the trays and filled the display cases to the brim.

"The hordes are packing in and Susie the mouth spotted Adams this morning, so she and her gossip queens have decided to watch the show." Hester slammed down some empty mugs.

"There will be no show, no fireworks. Think good thoughts."

"I don't think calm thoughts will help. Selling your recipe will." Marie Hestis stood before Lila in a slim-fitting business suit, heels, and well-coiffed blonde hair, with nary a strand out of place.

"Ms. Hestis, you and your obsession with my recipes aren't welcome in my bakery." Would this woman never give up?

Marie swept an arm around the densely packed bakery and pointed to the avid watchers. "Do you really want to make a scene in front of your patrons?" Marie leaned in and winked. "I see the esteemed Clifford Adams and his entourage are here.

Best of luck. A good review will boost your Decadent Death by Brownie's reputation and Hestia Wholesome Hits will make a bucket load when we buy your recipe."

Before Lila could shoot off a suitably sarcastic reply, the Hestia rep disappeared out the door.

"That woman makes me want to bake nails into a cake and feed it to her, one sharp bite at a time," Lila ground out.

"She doesn't seem so bad," Janie offered with a shamefaced shrug.

"That's the type of lady who will do anything to get what she wants, no matter the fallout." Hester pointed at Lila. "No more talking about feeding customers nails. That's a rumor we don't need."

Lila held up her hands. "Point taken." She glanced around the room. Everyone seemed happy enough. The atmosphere and the bakery felt warm and inviting. The good vibes-infused baking seemed to be doing the trick. Lila shuddered at the memory of the last time her witchy gifts had failed her. The food fight and bitter baked goods incident still traumatized her.

"Mr. Adams ate all of his brownie," Janie whispered to Lila. "It looks like he's writing something by the way he's slumped over. I think he's trying to hide what he wrote."

Lila focused on the food critic's table just as two middle-aged women sitting with him stood and left. Clifford was slumped to one side, one arm hiding his paper. Lila narrowed her gaze. The critic seemed way too quiet... Normally a grunter and tisker, this time he remained quiet... *Too quiet.* "Hester, call Braun and get that annoying reaper back here ASAP."

"Why?" Hester frowned, glancing around.

Janie took a step away from Hester and Lila, white faced. "It happened again, hasn't it?"

A shrill screech ripped the good vibes of the bakery to pieces as Susie Barnes stood and pointed to the food critic.

The late food critic...

ELEVEN

"So, this is the supernatural murder capital of the world? Charming." A wide-shouldered, baldheaded man, with the same hooked nose and gray eyes as Matthew Grim, nodded to Lila as he joined the other reaper in the bakery.

"Depends on whether you're the victim, I guess." Lila grimaced. "Since you're with Sir Nosy, I guess you're the reaper daddy?"

The older man snickered and elbowed Matthew. "Junior here has a nose for trouble and likes to know what's going on. We call him our trouble hound."

"Junior?"

"He's our youngest. Last baby bird to fly the coop, so to speak." The older man winked at Lila. "You look like your grandmother."

What a nasty thing to say. "That's not a compliment if you know Elspeth."

"Probably not, but she was a looker in her younger days. I'm Edwin Grim. Call me Ed." He extended a hand and gently took Lila's hand in his own. Ed scrutinized the witch. "You need more sleep."

"I need fewer dead bodies in my life." Lila disengaged her hand then flicked a look toward *Junior*. "Your dad is much nicer than you are."

Matthew grunted. "You aren't the first to say that." He turned to the Chief of Police. "What do we have, Zach?"

Zach Braun, Police Chief, stood and peeled off his latex gloves. "My crime scene. The technicians have already been over the area, so you can touch whatever you need to now." Braun nodded to the elder Grim. "Nice to see you again, Ed. Wish we had better news for you."

Lila butted in. "Considering it's my bakery, how about you tell me the news?"

"The news is Clifford Adams died of a heart attack."

"Phew. Let's my bakery off the hook." Lila beamed to the room. "That's a load off my witchy bones." Lila stuttered to a halt when Braun held a hand up.

"My healer gave Adams the once over. He had a pre-existing heart condition, but the heart attack was brought on by a dose of Ephedra."

Ed Grim nodded and tapped his chin with a forefinger. "It's a plant that causes heart palpitations and increases blood pressure. If he already had a bad heart, this would have easily killed him."

"But why? How? I swear, I'm not Elspeth. I didn't poison him."

"Someone did." Matthew crouched next to the body and used his scythe to turn Adams' palm over. "Same hexed incision on his palm as Henrietta Barnes. No soul." He glared up at his father. "Believe me now?"

Ed held up his hand. "Hey, I didn't disbelieve you, but Point Muse has a reputation. I needed to see the body to believe it."

"I. Didn't. Poison. Adams." Lila slammed her hand on the counter for emphasis. "I needed him to love my brownies, not die. Maybe he ingested the poison somewhere else?"

"No. My healer tested the food on the table. The icing had Ephedra powder present."

Lila slid down the counter until she reached the

floor. "I'm ruined. Ruined." Her wailing increased on the last word.

Matthew squatted next to Lila and pitched his voice low. "I wouldn't have picked a Harrow for a whiner and a quitter."

"Then you haven't known many. *Hey.*" Lila raised her head and glared at the reaper. "I am not a whiner or a quitter. I'm a small business owner. Reputation is everything. Not to mention, people will be too scared to eat here if they think they'll die."

"Then suck it up and help me find the killer." Matthew extended a hand to Lila.

Lila considered the pain-in-her-patootie reaper. Until now, she'd been a suspect, but something had pointed Grim junior away from her. "Why don't you think I'm the killer anymore?"

Matthew yanked Lila upright. "Too many of the clues point to you. It's too obvious. If you or any of the Harrows committed murder, I suspect we'd never find the body or any evidence of wrongdoing."

Lila dropped Grim's hand, ignoring the heat of his skin. She wiped the feel of his hand away on her jeans. "You aren't wrong. But if someone deliberately poisoned Clifford, how did they know he'd be here? I had no clue he'd decided to critique my brownie recipe today. How would anyone else have realized he'd be here?"

Grim senior walked over and tucked Lila's arm under his, strolling around the bakery like an old-fashioned promenading couple. "Now, dear, did anyone have any grudges against Mr. Adams?"

Lila snickered. "He's a food critic. Everyone loved to hate him. Mostly people ignored him." Lila frowned. "There were two women sitting with him, though. Probably early fifties. They left pretty much as we discovered he'd died."

Matthew and Braun exchanged a glance and a whispered conversation.

"Ever feel like you're been kicked out of the game?"

Ed patted Lila's hand. "Trust me, darling, the day any Harrow lets someone keep her from mayhem is the day she's ten feet under."

Grim elder had an interesting way of putting things, but he wasn't wrong.

"You three have some plans to make. I think I'll wander around Point Muse. Get a feel for the town." Ed saluted the now silent trio and headed out onto Main Street.

"Plan away, boys. But you better count me in and share what you know." Lila stood with hands on hips.

"Now, Lila." Braun stepped forward, but Matthew broke in before the Police Chief could say anything else.

"The two women may have been the Keres sisters, but someone knew Adams would be here. You said he was a food critic? Surely, whoever he wrote for would know his whereabouts?"

"The Point Muse Chronicles. They're just down the road."

"Lila and I will nose around the newspaper," Matthew told the Police Chief. "Call us if you get anything else."

Braun cleared his throat. "Will do. There's something else, Lila."

Lila braced a hand against the nearest solid object. Matthew Grim's muscled shoulder. "Do your worst, lawman."

"I'm sorry, but for the moment the bakery is closed. I want my team to go over the crime scene again."

"I figured." Lila blinked furiously. Even though she knew the closure was coming and was only temporary, it still hurt to think that her precious bakery would close the doors even if only for a day or two. "You better get on with it then. I don't want my sole remaining customers to wander off. Rose at

Mayweather Inn has even started serving cakes just to spite me."

"I'll see what I can do." Braun waved his crew of crime experts back in from the kitchen.

Matthew led Lila out onto Main Street. "I see you're hellhound free. Tell me your grandmother isn't puppy sitting?"

"Do I look certifiably insane?" Lila held up a hand. "Don't answer that. Nash is due a checkup. Mom's giving him the once over. Expect to see the puppy causing mayhem sometime soon."

"I had a feeling Point Muse is used to mayhem." Matthew looked up and down the bustling Main Street. "Lots of people out and about. Doesn't seem like the murders have affected local businesses at all."

"The gossips love a good murder, brings the customers out in droves, or is that a flock?" Lila snickered. Point Muse lived for gossip, the juicier the better. Except for the murder rate, the town was a pretty desirable place to live for supernaturals. The harborside town sported cobblestones, gables, and wood and stone buildings that exuded charm and sucked unwary supernatural travelers into extending their stay.

"I get the gossip thing." Matthew smiled politely

at a small group of middle-aged women who turned away once the reaper noticed them.

"Any of them look like the ladies you saw with Adams?"

Lila continued walking but shook her head. "Nope. Just the typical Point Muse cronies." She pointed to a white stone building with a dark roof. "That's the Chronicle. The editor, Percy, owns the building. Actually...," Lila qualified, "His mother owns the building. But she's retired to a beach somewhere, so Percy runs the newspaper. He's decent enough for a newshound. He's helped the Harrows out before but..."

"He's a reporter," Matthew added cynically. He grabbed the door to the paper and held it open for Lila.

Lila sailed through and sashayed up to the front reception desk. "Hey there, Macy. Percy in?" She braced herself for the saccharin tornado.

"Drama llama Lila. I haven't seen you in ages." A short, plump, brassy redhead flew out of her chair and wrapped hot pink talons around Lila's arms before yanking her into a swaying hug.

"We've talked about personal space before, Macy." Lila fought off the clinging and took a step back, bumping into Matthew. Taking this as a sign, she grabbed Matthew and shoved him under the redheaded bus. "Hey, Macy, have you met Matthew Grim? He's a friend of Zach Braun's and he's single." Lila threw in the last bit to chum the water and attract the Macy shark.

"Well now. *Hello there.*" The redheaded fluffed her hair and winked at the reaper. "Just what can I do for you, tall and handsome?"

Lila stifled a snicker. Tall and handsome looked as awkward as a teetotaler at one of Elspeth's karaoke nights.

He shoved his hands into his pockets and shuffled his feet as he looked to Lila for help.

Taking pity on the poor man, Lila stepped up again and slid an arm through Matthew's. "We need an urgent meeting with Percy."

"It's selfish not to share the fresh meat, Lila Harrow." Macy sniffed and tottered back to her chair on sharp black stilettos. "I don't know if I can fit you in last minute. Our editor is a very busy man. Especially with a murderer in town."

"We have information the editor may find interesting," Matthew found his voice.

"No doubt when you have a Harrow in tow. Bodies follow them around like puppy dogs. Always the center of drama, even in school," Macy sneered at Lila.

"Hey." Lila crossed her arms over her chest. "Those Chupacabras were not my fault."

"I suffered blood loss and spent a week in hospital. I missed the senior trip and had pasty white skin for months," Macy hollered back.

"All Holly's fault," Lila muttered mutinously as Matthew hushed her with a hand gesture.

"I'd really appreciate it, Macy, if we could get a little time with your editor."

"He has nicer manners then you do, Harrow." Macy consulted her diary. "The editor has five minutes free a week from tomorrow." She smiled spitefully at Lila. "That's the best I can do for you."

"Macy." Percival Hague, the editor of Point Muse Chronicles, stood off to the side of reception. "What did we talk about last week?"

Macy scraped her talons across the desk and spoke through gritted teeth, "Always call you when a Harrow tip comes through. There is always a story hanging around the Harrows like a bad spell."

"Not exactly my words, but the meaning's there." Percival stepped back and gestured to the duo to follow him into his office. He waved a hand at two stiff-backed chairs in front of his desk. "Sorry. You know how Macy feels about you, Lila."

"It's not my fault she spent a week in hospital after graduation and missed the senior trip."

"You did introduce the Chupacabras to the senior class."

"Holly's fault. If Macy hadn't drenched herself in lavender perfume, she'd have been fine. Everyone knows Chupacabras love lavender. She must've smelt like the best meal around town."

"Clearly not everyone knows about the Chupacabras' love of lavender." The reporter adjusted his black-rimmed glasses. "Nice to meet you, Mr. Grim. I'm Percival Hague. Chief editor and lone reporter for the Point Muse Chronicles. Call me Percy."

Matthew inclined his head. "Nice to meet you, Percy. The grapevine works well in Point Muse If you already know my name."

"The bane of every secretive person's life, but handy for a reporter."

Lila let the two men introduce themselves and tried to lean back in the posture-breaking chair. She looked around Percy's office. She'd never actually been here before. Pictures of Percy holding up Point Muse Academy's first school newspaper caught her attention. Percy Hague hadn't changed one bit. Still tall and skinny with short cropped brown hair. An average-looking guy who blended into the background. Sometimes deliberately. The more unobtrusive he seemed, the more information he squeezed out of you. "You haven't changed a bit, Percy."

Manly greetings done, Percy turned to Lila. "Neither have you. Still in the thick of chaos and mayhem, as always."

"Hey." Lila affected outrage. "Sometimes the mayhem works. Look at how we worked together to take down that Siren killer."

"Actually," Percy corrected Lila, "You used my papers to draw out the killer. Technically that was you using my skills and my paper, not us working together."

Lila waved a hand around. "Same difference. We need a favor, Percy. We need to find out who knew Adams was heading to my place to review my brownie."

"He had the space for a food review. I suggested your place. That's all."

"But why think of us now? Except for the Siren murder, we've had nothing to do with the Chronicle and we avoid Adams like the plague," Lila pressed

Percy. She had a witchy feeling there was more to the story.

"To be honest," Percy cleared his throat, "I received an anonymous phone call. The caller seemed to think there might be something wrong with your food. Only an expert like Clifford could track the issue down and he'd have the scoop if it were true. It was suggested Adams be sent to your bakery."

Matthew leaned forward, hands on knees, his face inscrutable. "Did you get their name?"

"No, and they blocked their call number as well. Drama follows Harrows, so I decided to send Clifford to review your brownies anyway."

"Why that recipe in particular?"

Percy answered the reaper without question, but with that big nose and his large shoulders, Matthew did cut an imposing figure.

"The whole town knows that Hestia Wholesome Hits is after your brownie recipe. I thought Clifford should try it. See what the fuss was about. I regret that decision now. Gossip runs like a wildfire through this town. Numerous people have contacted me already to let me know of Clifford Adams' demise." Percy slumped, his shoulders hunching. "Clifford wasn't the most lovable fellow, but he had a devoted following. I know I shouldn't be thinking about business right now, but I don't want my subscription numbers tanking." He tapped his fingers on the table, then paused and stared into space.

"No. Whatever you're thinking. Just no."

"Elspeth could be a perfect substitute."

"You've been sniffing witchshine." Lila stood and grabbed Matthew's arm, attempting to yank him up, but failing miserably. Instead, she overbalanced and would've fallen if Matthew hadn't grabbed her wrist. "Thanks. Now get up before Percy insists Elspeth not only becomes the new food critic but he also ropes her in to become a gossip columnist for the paper."

"Hey, that's a great idea." Percy snapped his fingers.

"She meddles enough in our lives as it is. Much more and we could end up in Elspethaggedon." This time when Lila grabbed Matthew's arm, he stood.

"Thanks, Percy." Lila waved to the reporter and hoofed it out, past Macy, ignoring the fuming receptionist. She pushed out onto Main Street and raised her face to the morning sun.

"The killer organized Adams to review your food and then took him out to frame you." Matthew strolled next to Lila as they headed back toward the bakery.

An itch started at the back of Lila's neck and traveled down her spine. She lifted her thick brown curly hair and scratched the skin underneath. "One of my customers managed to poison Clifford. Maybe those two women who sat with him?"

"Maybe. There's a few options we need to explore yet."

The itch niggled at Lila's neck again. As she walked, she took a quick glance around. A shadow darted from one doorway to another on the opposite side of the road. Frowning, Lila tried to track the shadow, but it evaporated. Still, the itching feeling persisted. *That was it.* Lila ground to a halt and pointed across the road. "Enough cloak and dagger. Hex up and show yourself." Lila waited a few seconds then stomped a foot. "I'll cut your sugar off if you don't show your face." She raised her voice again. "Right now, stalker."

"Lila? You okay?" Matthew spoke in a low calming voice.

"I'm not crazy if that's what you're asking."

"Good, because I'm a reaper, not an asylum attendant. Care to share what's running through your very busy head?"

"Someone was following me and rudely won't show themselves," Lila ground out, eyes trained on the street ahead of her.

Matthew scrutinized Main Street. "There's no one there now. Let's get back to your bakery."

"I'm not crazy." This time Lila pouted, her bottom lip puffed out. It was all Elspeth's fault. When any Harrow voiced an outlandish idea, everyone thought they were crazy. Just because of Elspeth's antics.

"Nope, not crazy. But you *are* a Harrow. Let's get back and avoid whatever magical mayhem is coming Point Muse's way."

"You may have a point, as much as it pains me to admit you're right. Lead on, Grim junior." Lila followed behind the reaper. Harrows had a tendency to attract chaos. But Lila had a horrible feeling the murders were more personally directed toward her than general Harrow carnage.

TWELVE

"How did you ditch the reaper and his daddy?"

"I waited until dinner and suggested Elspeth introduce Ed and his son to Harrow cuisine. Elspeth ran with the idea, and Aunt Winifred started lighting her candles. Once the cooking started, I bolted."

Holly fist-pumped Lila. "I like the reaper and all, but I'm glad you left them at home. You know what my bosses are like."

"Secretive, freaky and obsessed with death." Lila paused for a moment. "Hey, that describes you." She poked a finger into Holly's ribs.

Squeaking, Holly stepped around the gravestone to avoid her cousin. "This is my workplace. A little decorum, please."

Holly, part banshee, part witch, worked at Elysian Fields Funeral Home and Mortuary. Her bosses were twin necromancers descended from the Greek ferryman, Charon, who ferries souls to the underworld. The twins ran the funeral home and collected information and artefacts on anything death related. "Why are we dodging graves? Couldn't we come in the front through the nice manicured, body-free front yard?" Elysian Fields Funeral Home resembled a gleaming white Grecian temple. Soaring ceilings, strong columns, and lots of marble. Much nicer than ancient gravestones. Lila shuddered as she sidestepped a freshly filled grave. "Seriously. How do you sleep at night? This place would cause me nightmares."

Holly shrugged. "I find the atmosphere calming. Everyone's quiet, no Harrow chaos or Elspeth cackles."

"Except the walking dead at Archibald Penne's funeral."

"Momentary blip in the serenity." Holly took a series of worn stone steps two at a time until she stood on a cobblestone patio that led to a heavy wooden door. "Side entrance only. My bosses don't want anyone to know we're here." Holly grunted as she dragged the heavy door open and ushered Lila inside.

"You're saying we're undesirables?"

"The Harrow perchance for public chaos is well-known. We prefer our business and home not to be associated with that kind of publicity." Hillary stood just inside with a supercilious eyebrow raised.

Lila fought the shudder that seeing Holly's boss caused. Tall and curvy, with olive skin and straight black hair that cascaded down in two shining sheets, there was something about the woman that raised Lila's hackles. Both she and a twin brother, Hector, liked to dress as Victorian gothic wannabes. Velvet, frothy netting, and lace, all in black and that was just Hillary's twin brother. The siblings felt wrong to her Harrow bones.

"Thank you for coming so quickly, Holly." Hector rushed up and grabbed Holly's hands, raising them halfway to his lips before he dragged them down again. Red flushed his cheeks. "I remembered, see." He let Holly disengage her hands and turned to Lila. "She has a thing about germs and the human mouth."

Or a thing about freaky necromancers touching her skin. "How can we help you?"

"There's something we need to show you." Hillary led the cousins to another side door with her brother following close behind. The door opened onto the outside and a small stone wall and enclosed garden. She produced an old-fashioned key and unlocked the gate which led out to another smaller cemetery, softly illuminated by one lone outside light. In the early evening, the headstones with worn, engraved writing were barely legible. Gravestones lay at angles and long buried graves were turned over, fresh dirt gathering on the surface.

Holly gasped, hand to her mouth. "Body snatchers."

Hector shook his head. "Thankfully, not this time. It seems they just dug up some of the dirt and knocked over some of the gravestones."

"It's still desecration. Why on earth would anyone do this?"

Lila patted Holly on the back. "Calm down, cuz. No one stole a body or helped the dead to rise this time."

"Quite." Hillary sniffed. "That Dragon walking-dead debacle damaged our reputation. We don't want word of *this* incident getting out. Understand me, Harrows?"

Holly opened her mouth, but Lila stood on her foot to keep her quiet. "Happy to keep quiet. We need something in return."

"We assumed." Hillary eyed Lila like a bug under a microscope.

"We need any information you have on the Keres Daimons or reapers."

Hector waved his hand in the air. "I have research on both of those topics."

"Great. Here's a question, why call us about the dug-up graves?"

Hillary took charge of the conversation. "We heard the gossip about the bodies you found. Hector immediately went into research mode. When we saw the disturbed graves, we thought you should know as we think it involves you anyway."

Holly spoke in a low tone, her words dripping into a momentary pool of silence. "How does grave dirt affect Harrows?"

"Grave dirt can be a major component to quite a few spells. Hexes, love potions, cursing and necromancy." Hector took on a lecturing tone. "Even the Egyptians, and ancient Greeks, studied magic practices utilizing grave dirt."

"You think someone stole graveyard dirt to hex

us?" Holly gripped Lila's arm tight. "Maybe we should talk to Elspeth."

"Elspeth is one of our best customers and an expert in the field, but it isn't only the hexing and cursing that graveyard dirt can be used for. It's also a component in protection spells."

Lila grunted. "Either someone wants to date, kill or protect us?"

"Essentially. It's wonderful to be wanted." Hillary smirked at Lila's dumbfounded expression. "If you could excuse me, I have to organize a clean-up for the cemetery." Without a backward glance, Hillary flounced inside.

"If you follow me to my office, I'll dig out the research for you." Hector led the Harrows back inside the funeral home.

Lila drew Holly aside. "How can you stand working for those two? They give me the heebie-jeebies."

"Honestly, they aren't that bad. Except the habit Hector has of kissing my hand." Holly shuddered.

"Or the fact that they can call the dead?"

"Pfft." Holly waved Lila's words away. "They're trying to help us. Be gracious."

"If you'd like to come in?" Hector held the door open to his office.

With trepidation, Lila followed Holly inside...to complete chaos. Elspeth would have loved the office. Books lay in lopsided piles and covered every available surface. A stack of dark-stained wood shelves lined one wall and a display cabinet housed death trinkets Holly would drool over. Grotesque masks, canopic jars of Egyptian organs, mummified animals, bizarre jewelry and even the odd gold coin lay packed like sardines on the dusty shelves. Lila reached out a hand to a particularly shiny gold coin.

"I wouldn't do that if I was you. I don't think grandfather would be very impressed and he has a horrible temper. Just ask your father, Shade. They fight all the time."

Lila yanked her hand back. "Sorry if it's some family antique. And as I caught my father visiting my mom in a bathrobe, I'm not currently talking to him."

Hector cleared his throat. "I don't really have a reply to the image of your father in a bathrobe. But those coins are obol or obolos. The dead pay Charon, my grandfather, to transport them to Hades and the underworld. When we were young, grandfather used to do magic tricks with them. He was quite talented." Hector gestured to two wooden chairs buried under loose papers. "Please sit. Just dump the papers onto the floor."

Taking the packrat at his word, Lila shoved the papers off.

Holly, not so cavalier, gently placed the papers next to her feet.

Not waiting for her cousin to speak, Lila plunged in. "What have you got for us?"

"I spoke to my grandfather. He knows the Daimons quite well. Especially Stygere, they used to date. He was quite saddened to hear she'd died a human death. But I guess that's an occupational hazard in his line of work. Dealing with people dying."

"Stygere?" Did the necromancer mean Geri?

"Yes. The one you called Geri. The Daimons' names in chronological age are Stygere, Anaplekte and Achlys, or Geri, Ana and Lys. As you know, they were Daimons, female death spirits. They were drawn to violent death. The nastier the better. They were supposed to eat the hearts of the slain, then use the dagger of Degmon to siphon the souls and deliver them to Hades."

"But they got greedy?" Holly finally joined in.

"Essentially. Charon said that Ana and Lys plotted to keep the souls to maintain a youthful appearance. Geri went along for a while, then reported them to Hades and was given witness protection as a human. The other sisters were imprisoned within Tartarus."

"The old girls wanted to look non-saggy, so they turned against Hades? Why not just have plastic surgery?"

Hector shot Lila a disapproving glance.

"Their natural appearance is of wasted hags with claws and gnashing teeth. It's not unsurprising they have body image issues."

Immortal death spirits with body issues, not something she'd expected to hear. Lila leaned forward. "Can you tell me anything else about the sisters that might help?"

"They hold a grudge well and can't stand your father. As Hades' chief enforcer, he doesn't have the best reputation with those he drags back to Tartarus."

"Plus, he cheats at cards," Holly offered.

"That's my dad."

"And he still cheats, he's as bad as Elspeth."

"No one is as bad as Elspeth." Lila matched Holly's identical shudder. Elspeth left a lasting impression and a foul taste in the mouth when she went full poker hag. No one was safe. "The sisters are holding a grudge and want to be young again. So, they headed here to get the dagger and revenge against Geri. Why stay now, instead of running? And why frame me?"

"At a guess from what my grandfather has said, this is about your father and toying with their prey."

"Great. I'm a chew toy." Lila angled her head back and winced as the wooden chair refused to give.

"Essentially. The rumor mill already noted the presence of two reapers from Grim Inc. They're a very well-known family in death circles. Honorable and respectful and with a reputation for being incorruptible. "

"We'll see what Elspeth says about that," Lila muttered under her breath. "Any specifics?"

"Not really. The youngest reaper has a high clearance rate and a reputation for being more flexible than the rest of his family. That help at all?"

Lila grunted but forced a smile as Holly kicked her on the leg. "Thanks for your help, Hector."

"I'm always happy to help Holly's family. I suggest speaking to Elspeth about the gravedigger. She may be able to advise on countermeasures." Hector stood behind his desk. "Holly knows the way out."

Taking her boss's hint, Holly grabbed Lila and

dragged her out of the office. "They help pay my bills. Be a little nicer next time."

"What bills? You live in the house Elspeth owns. Your mother buys your food. What bills could you have?"

Holly blushed. "I may have a bobble head figure addiction. It comes at a cost."

Lila followed Holly out the back of the funeral home. She might not be able to pick her family, but she could pick her friends and allies. Maybe Matthew Grim and his reaping family could be both...

Maybe.

Messy enemies were the pits. At the very least after searching her apartment, they could've cleaned up. Lila toed a recipe book closed and groaned. She'd have to get professional cleaners in or let Elspeth loose with a cleaning spell. "I guess I now know where the graveyard dirt went, and it wasn't into a love potion." But was the mess in her apartment supposed to be a curse or protection? Her lovely somewhat-clean home had been torn apart. Recipe books lay in ripped piles around the room. Furniture turned over, linen and cushions shredded.

"At least they left my clothing and Nash's bed alone." Red heat flushed upward from her stomach, a rising tide that threatened to explode from her mouth in an expletive-laden tirade. Lila bit her tongue to keep the words inside. Instead, she indulged in a foot-stamping to make herself feel better. "Pointless losing my temper. I need to find the killer and make *them* clean this mess up." She kicked a cushion decorated with devilish cupcakes but froze when she heard a thump from her bedroom.

The tribal pounding in her ears almost overwhelmed her until her fight or flight instinct kicked in. Lila scuttled back to the front door and quickly switched the light off, plastering herself against the wall. If they couldn't see her, they couldn't hurt her. Of course, now she couldn't see them either. Lila smacked her forehead with a hand. *Idjit.*

Since her curtains were open, the moon, although not full, highlighted parts of her living room. Now her eyes had adjusted, she spotted familiar shapes as well as the hooded figure that loomed in her bedroom doorway. Lila slid down the wall slowly and patted the ground until she found a pile of recipe books. Using the wall as a guide, she stood, hefting the books in her hand. She readied herself.

The intruder moved forward a few steps and cursed as they collided with an upturned chair.

Lila gauged the area where the noise had originated from and let fly with a heavy cookbook. The figure yelped as Lila hit her target dead on. "Ha. You thought you could trash my place, whoever you are. But you'd be wrong. Vengeance is mine sayeth the baker." Lila lobbed another book at the intruder, who dodged with a whispered curse.

Feeling brave, Lila took a step away from the wall. "You're dealing with a worked-up Harrow. Prepare to grovel and clean my apartment after you confess to murder, you despicable cupcake hater." Lila grabbed another handful of small books and let fly with a barrage of gourmet bombs. Judging by the pained sounds, some hit the target.

But the intruder quickly retaliated with their own literary missiles. Lila braced herself for incoming fire but cheered when the book seemed to veer off and pepper around her instead of meeting Harrow flesh. "Take that, you rabid apartment destroyer." Lila tap-danced on the spot, sneezing, when a cloud of dust flew up into her face. She looked down and realized she stood upon a pile of graveyard dirt. *Aha,* maybe the dirt was meant to protect her instead of cursing or hexing her. *But who would steal graveyard dirt to protect her?*

The door to Lila's apartment flew open and both Lila and her apartment-destroying nemesis froze. Matthew Grim surged inside, his scythe extended to full length.

"Matthew, watch out." Lila tried to warn him about the state of her apartment, but it was too late. The reaper tripped over a small table and flew through the air, snagging Lila along the way. She groaned as Matthew's hard body collided with hers and took them both down.

Matthew twisted so he hit the ground first, letting out a pained grunt as Lila collapsed against his chest.

The intruder jolted forward, jumped over the obstacles, and fled the apartment.

A muffled howl echoed up the stairs, along with the thump of multiple feet.

Lila adjusted her weight as Matthew groaned. "I did tell you to wait."

"I thought you were in trouble. I heard all the thumps on the floor from my place."

"Book missiles. I had the intruder cornered until you blundered in."

"Rescuing, not blundering."

"I'm a Harrow. We rescue ourselves." Lila squirmed as something hard poked her in the side. "I see size does matter."

"That's my scythe," Matthew growled.

"I'm aware of what it is since it's boring a hole into my side. Care to remove it?"

Grim slid his scythe off to the side and out of Lila's way.

"Lila Marie Harrow. Put that man down immediately. You have no clue where he's been."

Her mother's strident tones filled the room, along with a blaze of light as someone flicked the light switch.

Another howl sounded from just outside the apartment moments before Nash pounded in, eyes bright red and his body swelled to twice his size. He took a running leap and landed next to Lila, slathering her face in slightly singeing doggy kisses.

"Don't ask the girl to put him down. This could be her only chance not to end up a sour old spinster. Maybe we should bind them together right now." Elspeth cackled and the bulbs in the hallway outside the apartment shattered in a low-tech tinkle of glass.

Lila lowered her head onto Grim's warm

muscled chest with a heavy thump. "Smother me in sugar and deep fry me right now. I'm done."

"That's the way to catch a lady, son. Top notch job." Ed Grim's sarcastic tones joined Elspeth's cackling.

"Can you deep fry me too? He'll never let me live this down." Matthew groaned as Ed and Elspeth squabbled over who'd protect Lila better. The Grims or the Harrows.

"Do you think we could sneak off?" Lila lifted her head and rested her chin on Matthew's chest, staring into his laughing gray eyes. Matthew expelled a long breath, causing Lila's head to bob up and down like one of Holly's bobble head figures.

"I think that ship sailed the same time we landed here."

Ed and Elspeth's squabbling escalated to shouting and finger-pointing. "Does your father realize he can't win against my grandmother?"

"Never admit defeat is the family motto."

"Never get caught is ours." Lila sighed and contemplated her trashed apartment. The Harrow family might drive each other crazy, but they were always there to protect and defend.

"Now they're arguing about where you'd be the most protected. My apartment or Harrow House."

"No way, no how, am I moving back into Harrow house. That way lies insanity and possibly another murder." She'd rather face the book-dodging killer than live with her family's special brand of chaos and mayhem.

Family life could be murder...

"How did they talk me into moving into Harrow House?" Lila kicked out her unicorn slippers and considered her fuzzy purple pajama pants.

"From what I hear, you were too busy nuzzling the reaper's chest to dredge up an argument." Xandie crunched on a crispy piece of bacon. "Aunt Winifred's bacon rocks my world."

"Hey." Lila poked her cousin with the tip of one unicorn slipper. "There was no nuzzling involved and yes, Aunt Win's bacon is amazing."

Xandie swallowed her last morsel of bacon and licked her fingers. "Your apartment got trashed by a mysterious shadowy figure, I hear. Any idea what they were after?"

"Not a clue. The Keres sisters already have that

dagger thingy. I have no idea what else they were after."

"Maybe you just annoyed them, and it was a temper tantrum? I can sympathize. You *are* pretty irritating," Holly pointed out helpfully.

"I'm an absolute peach. I put up with the rest of you, don't I?"

"Along with all the beating of chest and gnashing of teeth. Our little drama llama." Darius Shade, Lila's father, patted his daughter's head.

Lila shuddered and closed her eyes. "Dad, this isn't mom's house. Why are you still wearing a bathrobe? Doesn't Hades pay you enough to buy clothing?"

"Oh, sweetie. Your shyness is adorable." Shade pinched Lila's cheeks. "And we *all* had a Harrow sleepover last night. You know that."

Shoving her father's hands away from her cheeks, Lila grumped, "I tend to block out traumatic events."

"You get that from me. I'm still blocking the image of my baby lying on top of a strange reaper."

"We should all be that lucky," Holly murmured.

"What was that, Holly bean?" Shade cocked an eyebrow at his niece.

Holly grabbed another slice of bacon and

crammed it in her mouth, mumbling around the food, "Nothing, Uncle Shade."

He winked. "I didn't think so."

"Now, Shade. Please stop teasing the children. We'd given up hope Lila would find anyone to take her on." Winifred dumped another load of crunchy bacon onto a plate in the middle of the kitchen table.

Lila went into a coughing fit, the bacon she'd just swallowed lodged in her throat.

Xandie obliged with a bang of the hand to Lila's shoulder blades. The offending piece of food flew out and landed onto the table.

"Thanks, Aunt Winifred, but please don't help me again, it traumatizes me." Lila slumped down into a chair. The whole family, a.k.a. the meddling aunts, despaired of getting their daughters hooked up. Point Muse had slim pickings of the opposite sex when you'd changed the nappies of the younger male generation and watched those of your own circle go through the awkward teenage stage. Besides, Winifred wasn't exactly overflowing in the boyfriend apartment either. Aunt Win, the shortest of the three sisters, had brassy red hair and the amber Harrow eyes. She also tended to the plump side, whereas Lila's mother and Xandie's mom, Miranda, were taller and more angular. Winifred ran the local candle and potion store and had the biggest heart of all the Harrows.

"She's just telling it like it is, doll face." Colin, Elspeth's talking food-obsessed pug, wandered in. He perched on the floor and scratched his tummy. "Hey Winnie? Sweetie, babe? Where's my breakfast? Got a powerful hunger brewing."

That wasn't all Colin brewed. His bodily functions were famous for their radioactive levels. He could clear a room faster than any Elspeth-related hex.

Lila snatched another piece of bacon before Winifred slid the pile of freshly cooked bacon onto another plate that she deposited at a place setting. She held out a chair. "All ready, dear. Remember your table manners."

"Yeah. No puddles, or bodily functions, at the table. I got you, sweet cheeks." Colin scrambled onto a chair and wolfed his portion of the bacon down.

"Winifred," Amelia hollered as she stomped into the kitchen, followed by Nash. "We talked about this. Colin is a dog, not a person. No feeding at the table and certainly not bacon." Amelia swiped the bacon plate, swapped it for a pile of dry dog food and placed the plate on the floor. "Colin's diet does not need added fats.

"Man. The food police just arrived." Colin slunk to the floor and nibbled on a dog biscuit. He spat it out with extreme prejudice. "Are you trying to kill me? Is this a devious ploy to get rid of Elspeth's favorite child?"

Lila snickered. "You can keep that position. No one wants to spend enough time with Elspeth to qualify as her favorite."

The trill of the phone echoed somewhere in Harrow House. Winifred rushed out to grab it. The kitchen table shook as the floor underneath vibrated. After generations of Harrows had lived here, Harrow House developed a sentient, nosy mind of its own. Walls would move and doors closed for no reason except to amuse the house. Occasionally, the house would help as long as gossip was involved. The house thrived on drama just like the rest of the family.

Nash pushed out from behind Amelia and sniffed, his eyes glowing faintly red, nose twitching like mad. He whined from next to the counter and stared soulfully up at the plate of bacon.

Colin grimaced and tried another biscuit. "Give it up, mate. That woman is hard. Hard, mean, food police. The bacon is a lost cause."

Nash focused on the plate. A single rasher of

bacon wobbled and slid off, scooting along the counter until it dropped into Nash's open mouth.

The occupants of the kitchen stared open-mouthed at the hellhound.

"I can foresee a beneficial relationship between the two of us, hound. Hang with me and food heaven will be assured." Colin winked. "Now, how about you set me up?" Colin closed his eyes and opened his mouth wide, drool hanging on the corner of his doggy mouth.

Nash obliged and a handful bacon slid across the bench into Colin's mouth like a food tsunami.

Lila snapped her mouth shut. "Mom?"

Amelia banged a coffee mug down on the bench. "There isn't enough coffee in the day to deal with this." She pointed a finger at her snickering husband. "This is your fault. Yours and Hades'. I blame you both equally."

Shade held up a hand. "This is for our daughter's protection, sweetness. Besides, Nash is the runt of the litter. We have no clue what gifts he'll have."

"Stealing bacon and aiding and abetting Colin's devious food habits is not a gift." Amelia glared at her husband.

"Yeah, who'd have thought a maniacal talking

pug would corrupt an impressionable, young, hell-hound puppy." Lila high-fived Xandie.

"At least Colin doesn't sing karaoke." Xandie shuddered. "Theo bought his own karaoke machine off Witchbay. It's enchanted to turn on when it hears his voice. Now I hear high-pitched love ballads at all times of the day and night."

"See." Holly pointed at the dogs. "This is why I'll remain animal free. No pets, familiars, or any kind of animal I have to feed. Animal free zone."

Winifred appeared in the doorway, notepad in hand. "Girls, I have a message from Rose at Mayweather Inn. If you're free, she'd like to see you this morning."

Lila choked back a laugh. "I'm pretty sure Rose didn't put her request quite like that."

"No, she actually said... Tell Lila I'll drop the cake if she gets her too wide patootie down to the Inn ASAP." Winifred cleared her throat. "I for one think you're perfect, dear. There's no body shaming in our circle of peace."

"Speaking of body shaming... When a pug's gotta go, a pug's gotta go. I knew that dry stuff was no good for me." Colin wiggled like a dervish until a peaceful expression spread across his puggish face.

Like clapped a hand over her mouth and shoved

Holly and Xandie to the floor in her rush to avoid the cloud of radioactive flatulence spreading across the room.

When it came to Colin, it was every Harrow for herself.

"I tell you. There's something Harrow weird about those women. I don't want any of my other customers exposed."

"Being a Harrow isn't a communicable disease," Xandie pointed out.

"Librarian has big words. But true." Lila bit back a chuckle at the expression on Rose's heavily made-up face. Rose Mayweather, owner and proprietor of Mayweather Inn, just happened to be a descendant of Aphrodite and obsessed with the nineteen fifties. The Inn owner decked herself out in fifties style dresses with matching bouffant hairdos. She also hated the Harrows. She and Elspeth had an ongoing feud neither would back down from.

"Deal with the weird, Harrows. *Before* my temper and my business fails. Plus, I'll forget my morning tea special. No competition with your bakery then. It's a win-win deal."

"No one's buying the cakes?"

Rose huffed. "There's no accounting for taste. Now get in there and deal with those women." Rose flounced off to reception.

Lila peered into the bar area of the Inn. "What's so weird about women drinking?"

Xandie pointed to one of the women. "Well, to start with, they just added salt to their lattes."

"You'd be shocked at some of the strange things people add to their beverages. I'm a baker, I've seen everything."

"Probably." Xandie peered at the two women sitting next to each other in a booth near the windows. "You see them in town before?"

The women, who looked to be in their thirties, wore an eclectic mismatch of clothing. One of the women wore skintight pink leggings, paired with black shorts and a loose blue T-shirt with the yellow vest. The other woman wore a blood-red pencil skirt with a pair of waterproof boots, and a fluffy Christmas sweater. Both women had long dark hair and painted nails. "Okay, they look a tad freaky, but they're probably just tourists."

"Maybe."

Xandie didn't sound convinced. Lila straightened. Time to show her cousin her own sleuthing prowess. "Let's ask them." She sauntered into the bar, ignoring Xandie's hisses. Lila made a beeline for the women, spotting that nasty Hestia rep in the far corner as she did. "Why can't that woman just leave town?"

"She can smell blood in the water. It attracts all kinds of predators." The woman with the pink leggings pointed to the seat across from her. "I can't believe I'm finally meeting you." She turned to her friend. "This is so exciting, isn't it, Lys?"

The other woman rolled her eyes. "You get excited about anything, Ana. Why don't you tell your little friend to stop eyeballing and join us instead?"

Lila turned and spotted Xandie behind a large plant in the corner of the bar. Honestly, with those non-existent hiding skills, how did her cousin solve anything? Lila gestured for Xandie to come and join them. "Sorry, my cousin's the Librarian. She has issues."

"Too much gas?" Ana nodded. "I hear it's a common human problem. That's okay, we don't judge."

Lys snorted. "Speak for yourself. I'm happy to judge."

Ana shushed her sister as Xandie joined them.

Lila and Xandie slid into the booth opposite the women.

"Now baker and Librarian, how can we help you?" Ana tucked her hands underneath the table and sat up primly.

"Who are you and why are you in Point Muse?" Lila probed bluntly.

"Way to be subtle, cousin." Xandie nudged Lila.

Lys shrugged. "We don't do subtle. We like our actions to be upfront, personal and easily understood."

"Just two sisters visiting this lovely town. A holiday of sorts. Been a very long time since we managed time off for good behavior." Ana beamed at the cousins.

"And now here we are, meeting Lila Harrow and the Librarian. It's really been quite an educational break so far."

Rose might be right. These two were definitely not playing with a full deck. "How do you know me? I'm just a baker."

Lys slapped the table, her red nails gouging furrows in the tabletop. "You're famous where we're from. Everyone knows the Harrow name." She leaned forward. "Is it true Elspeth Harrow's wanted by every government in the world and five religions have her noted down as a corrupting influence?"

Lila shrugged. "Probably, knowing my grandmother."

"Really, this world is so much fun now." Ana smiled sweetly at Xandie. "And of course, everyone's heard of the Librarian and her exploits."

"That's reassuring. I thought you might have forgotten about me when you sized up Lila." Xandie stared dead-faced at the two women.

"Don't worry." Ana patted Xandie's hand. "You're an important part of the team. You all are. Sometimes it's hard to see the pattern through the puzzle. Don't worry, Lila can help with that."

"Sooner rather than later." Lys winked at the girls. "Those slow on the uptake tend to not survive."

Lila placed both hands on the table. "That a threat?"

"Depends how you take it, little baker." Lys bared slightly pointed teeth at Lila.

"Now, sister. Poor Lila has enough threats to deal with right now." Ana stared earnestly at Lila. "Just remember. Not everything is as it seems." She stopped to consider her words for a moment, frowning, until a vague sunny smile spread across her face. "Then again, it could be as you see it. Depends on your point of view." She clapped her hands. "That's what makes this world so much fun, doesn't it, sister?"

"Whatevs." Lys ignored everyone at the table and picked at the side of her nail.

"Exactly." Ana looked pleased with herself.

"Now we've got that sorted, we have to go. Got a baker to cook or is that cake? I forget." Ana trilled a laugh and dragged her sister out of the booth. "Tootles, little baker and Librarian. See you soon."

Lila watched the insane duo squabbling and shoving each other as they left the bar. "Do you feel more confused or less now we've spoken to them?"

"I'm fairly certain their sanity levels are fluid, if that helps," Xandie offered.

"I guess insanity is a given when you're an immortal death hag prison escapee on the run from an ancient God jailer."

"The Keres's Daimons." Xandie nodded.

"Got it in one. It amazes me they managed to agree enough to kill anyone."

"They're getting younger every time they use that dagger."

Lila nodded. "Last time I heard them in Geri's shop they sounded like really old desiccated hags. In the retirement home, they just seemed like elderly ladies. Today they're in their mid-thirties. Everybody they eliminate makes them younger."

"But why waste time warning you about threats? Why not just kill you? And what's all that stuff about the great Lila Harrow?"

Xandie might be right. Something else was definitely going on. "I have no clue. The whole situation's freaky strange."

"Is this a work break? Or a business break?" Marie Hestis smiled at Lila. Her bright red glossy lipstick looked like a smear of red clown paint.

"Momentary pause before we get the surge. Why are you still in town?"

Marie sniffed. "Maybe I'm sourcing alternative recipes for Hestia? You aren't the only baker in town. "

"Actually, I am. But if you're talking about Rose's cakes, you might want to book into the hospital for food poisoning."

"I don't answer to you, Ms. Harrow. Besides, from what I hear, your bakery won't be around much longer," Marie sneered. "Hestia's offer doesn't last forever, and neither will you." The rep stormed off through the bar.

Xandie regarded her cousin. "I think that makes you two for two on the threat-o-meter."

Lila waved Xandie's concern away. "That's nothing for a Harrow. It's when everything goes quiet that you need to worry."

And she had a feeling that quiet time was just around the corner...

FOURTEEN

"Who did you bribe or kill?"

Lila poked her tongue out at her mouthy banshee cousin. "Neither one, if you must know. Braun okayed me to clean the bakery and prepare our stock. I'm still closed right now, but he'll clear me to open later today or tomorrow." Lila pumped a fist into the air. "Wahoo, Heart's Delight Bakery back in business. Take that, Hestia." She chortled and twitched her hips in a victory twerk.

Holly covered her eyes. "Your Elspeth moves are scarring. Please stop."

Giving one last twerk, Lila settled down. "I just don't want anything else to go wrong." She held up her hands. "My fingers are actually itching to bake. I called Hester and Janie in to get cleaning and prep started." Lila checked her watch. "Speaking of Janie, she should be here already. I'll go check the alley; she parks out there sometimes."

With a skip to her step, Lila opened the alley door and poked her head out. Janie's silver and blue moped sat parked in the alley, but her bakery assistant had disappeared. Lila stepped into the alley, pausing when she heard a low murmur.

She spotted Janie at the mouth of the alley and opened her mouth to yell out, but something muted her vocal cords for a moment.

"I told you. I won't do it anymore. It's wrong and she's nice." Janie paced up and down. "I don't care how deep in I am. She's a good person and you aren't." Janie's back stiffened and Lila scooted behind her bakery door, listening as Janie's voice grew louder as she moved closer.

"Don't you threaten me. You have more to lose than I do," Janie hissed into her phone before hanging up and throwing it to the ground. She sighed and picked it up again.

Lila pretended to come out through the alley door. "There you are. Ready to get started?"

"Yep." Janie jolted and forced a smile. "Ready and raring to go. And I swear, I won't muck things up anymore."

"If you're in trouble, you can talk to me." Lila stared at Janie for a moment. "I'm a Harrow, and we protect what's ours. You work for me, Janie. If you need it, the Harrows will protect you."

Janie's face crumpled. "That means a lot, Lila. More than I deserve." Janie blew out a breath and straightened. "I got myself into this mess, I'll get myself out." She offered a small smile. "I promise not to dump any more cake mixes on the floor."

Lila dropped the subject. For the first time since she'd hired the girl, Lila felt the real Janie had just spoken. "Okay. But I'm here if you need me." Lila waited for Janie's nod before continuing, "We have a delivery to drop off. Braun's okayed it. So, how about you take the van and do the drop-off?" Lila dangled the van's keys in Janie's delighted face.

"Really? My first time driving the van on a delivery." Janie snatched the keys and spun on the spot, squealing. She sobered up. "You won't regret this, I swear it."

"The delivery's already packed up on my bench ready to go. The station needs an order of honey cakes ASAP." Lila rolled her eyes. "Bears and honey. Who knew Point Muse law enforcement could be so bribable?"

"You're the boss. Police station it is." Janie slipped inside, whistling.

Whatever trouble had hold of Janie, she'd made a decision to step away. The girl's whole demeanor had changed. A heavy pile of weight had rolled off her shoulders and it showed. Lila grinned as she stepped back into the kitchen and watched Hester and Janie bustling around, ferrying the order out to the bakery van. *Good to be back in business, finally.* Even if she was only defrosting and heating honey buns for the police. Maybe things had turned around. "The van has touchy brakes. Remember, she's my pride and joy," Lila hollered at the door as her excited assistant rushed out.

Janie grinned and waved Lila off before carefully backing out of the alley.

"That girl looks like someone gave her a dozen cupcakes and a promotion." Hester grabbed a broom and gave the kitchen floor a quick swipe.

"I think she finally made a decision about an issue she had. Kind of freeing, I guess."

"Good. Maybe she'll stop dropping things now."

Nash pounded into the kitchen, panting.

"What's riled you up?" Hester crouched down and stared into the hellhound's eyes. "He ain't happy about something, but he hasn't gone full hellhound and flamed his eyes out yet." The Brownie straightened. "Better take him for walkies in case he needs to do his business. Last thing we need is some health code violation to do with smoking hellhound wee."

Sighing, Lila whistled to Nash and headed outside. Sometimes it felt like the Brownie owned the bakery, not her. Of course, Hester *had* been with the family for decades.

"That puppy taking you for walkies, girl?" Elspeth popped out of the hairdresser's, *Hair Today, Gone Tomorrow*. Owned by two of her gossiping cronies.

"Hester ordered me out of the bakery until Nash calmed down. She's worried about accidental puppy discharges."

Elspeth grimaced. "That's a nasty image." She linked arms with her granddaughter and strolled along Main Street.

Lila's witchy hackles rose. No way would Elspeth be this nice unless she wanted something. "Right, spit it out. I can't handle the tension. What do you want?"

"Can't a loving grandmother spend time with a favorite granddaughter?"

They looked at each other and burst out laughing. Elspeth wiped the tears from her face and waited for Lila's hiccups to subside. "Too hard to keep a straight face. Haven't had a belly laugh like that in a while." She straightened her iridescent green and blue shoulder-length wig and got down to business. "You need to get rid of my daughter from Harrow House."

"You have three daughters. Which one, and how permanently do you want to get rid of her?" Considering it was Elspeth she was talking to, it was a valid question.

"Your nosy, straitlaced mother and her bathrobe-hogging sperm donor of a husband."

"Eew, Elspeth. *Images.* Mom and dad will leave soon. Mom won't be able to stand the chaos for much longer and Hecate knows Hades can't do without Dad for too long."

Elspeth directed Lila across the road as they headed for the harbor and a small green park. "Her sanctimonious no bacon rule is ruining my morning. Poor Colin's wasting away. Get. Her. Out." Elspeth glared at her granddaughter.

Lila sighed. "Until this killer is caught, they won't move. At least Mom won't. Dad could disappear at any stage."

"Find the miscreant or I'll have to take measures."

Which could mean anything from a single hex to a supernatural nuclear strike, Elspeth style. Maximum carnage, maximum mayhem. All benefiting her grandmother. "I'll do my best; I'd hate for you to be put out because the killer's framing me."

"Hold that sass, girl. Remember the underwear drawer incident?" Elspeth waggled her fingers at her granddaughter and little pink and blue flickers played over her knuckles.

"Which one? All the underwear hexing has bled into one continuous nightmare of grandma knickers."

"Such lip from a dutiful granddaughter. Where is that Hades-ridden hellhound of yours?"

Lila took a glance around Harbor Park. The Council, in their infinite wisdom, had established a beautiful green space at the mouth of the harbor. Unfortunately, Elspeth spoiled it when she erected a stone statue of herself during her tyrannical period as Mayor. Since dictator Elspeth had been deposed in a town-sanctioned coup, no one had been brave enough to knock it down. Lila spotted Nash near the statue, leg raised. She closed her eyes in horror. Nothing would distract the tornado of outrage that was about to descend, Elspeth style.

"Don't. You. Dare. Hound," Elspeth screeched,

hands flapping overhead as she tried to distract the puppy from his bodily functions.

Nash dropped his leg and backed up, whining. His eyes flamed red and he angled his head back and howled.

A screech of tires came from the road. A blue van careened down the road and mounted the curb, barreling into the park.

Nash bolted from next to the statue and narrowly avoided the speeding van. Lila gasped, hands to mouth. She recognized the van and the terrified girl at the wheel heading straight toward the Elspeth statue.

Lila grabbed her grandmothers' arm and screamed, "Do something. That's Janie driving."

Elspeth's face settled into stone. "I'm sorry. It's too late. There's nothing I can do."

The sound of metal crunching into stone echoed through the park. Two women standing nearby immediately surged to the van and wrenched open the driver's door.

Lila released her hold on Elspeth's arm. Her whole body shook, and she wrapped her arms around herself.

"I'm sorry, Lila. It was too late for Janie." Elspeth extended a hand to her granddaughter.

Lila sidestepped. "What's the point of being the wicked witch of Point Muse if you can't use your powers when you need to."

Elspeth shook her head sadly. "Some things are a fixed point and have to happen."

Shaking her head, Lila moved toward the van. A group had already gathered around.

"Sweetie, you don't want to see her like that." Winifred stepped in front of Lila and maneuvered her away.

"Is she..." Lila couldn't bring herself to finish the sentence.

"She is. I'm sorry, Lila. Two women have already left to grab the police. Zach should be here any second."

Lila fought the tears back. Poor Janie. Whatever the girl had been involved in, she'd stood her ground and said no. Whoever had been on the other end of the phone had decided Janie was a loose end to be snapped. "Hang on. Did you say *two* women left to get help? What did they look like?"

Lila's aunt frowned. "In their thirties, I think, but dressed quite strangely. Very mix and match."

Ana and Lys. Strangely dressed described them to a tee. "Is there anything on Janie's hand? A cross or scratch?"

Winifred bit her lip. "I don't know. I didn't notice."

Maybe the Keres Daimons had struck again. Too much of a coincidence for someone else connected to her or her bakery to die and not have the demons involved. Those hags were going down.

"Lila, you shouldn't be here. You need to head to the bakery or Harrow house and lay low." Zach Braun, Police Chief, stepped up next to Lila.

"It was those hags. I'm sure of it." Lila clenched her fists at her side.

Nash sidled up to Lila and rubbed against her leg, whimpering.

"Have an open mind, Lila. We'll catch whoever's responsible. For now, you need to leave before the situation gets out of hand."

Zach made a point of glancing around them.

Lila followed his stare. Small groups of quietly whispering Point Muse residents were currently shooting her quick suspicious glances.

Braun might be right about her vacating the crime scene.

The whispering crowd in the park looked like it might be Harrow tar and feather time in Point Muse.

Lila was starting to feel like Elspeth...

FIFTEEN

"Hit me again, Hester." Lila slammed her mug down on the kitchen island and blinked furiously.

"I'm cutting you off, Harrow. You need to be able to focus and four cups of hot chocolate in a row will sugar-overdose you or send you to the bathroom."

Lila slumped against the island. "Even the Brownie has turned on me. Next thing, Point Muse will run me out of town just like my grandmother." She tapped her fingers morosely on the stone bench top. *Mind you,* the town had put up with Elspeth's antics for decades now, and her grandmother had only been run out of town by a furious mob a few times. Surely Lila had a little more time left before that happened.

"Stop feeling guilty like you caused that girl's

death. The van hit your grandmother's statue. That could happen to anyone."

"Somehow, I don't think so."

"I for one have had enough of your moping. Got a job for you." Hester flicked the dishrag at Lila. "You need to clean out Janie's locker. It has to be done."

"Braun will want to search it. Better if I don't touch it. I might break something anyway."

"Stop whining." Hester pointed at Lila. "Enough with the pity party. Get a clue. Literally. Put gloves on and search her locker yourself. Sleuthing might make you feel better."

Lila perked up. Hester was right. Janie may have left some kind a clue about the person she'd been on the phone to this morning. Faking indifference, because it never paid to tell Hester she was right, Lila stood and grabbed a pair of latex gloves from a drawer. "I guess I should at least take a look. Nash is under the island, could you keep an eye on him? We don't want him rolling in icing sugar again."

Hester waved Lila off.

Once Hester turned away, Lila hotfooted it to the tiny break room where a few staff lockers stood. Point Muse being the small town it was, no one locked anything, and Janie's locker was no exception.

"Thanks for making it easy, Janie. I won't let you down."

A momentary pain squeezed Lila's throat. The poor girl barely had a chance for a new life in Point Muse and now she wouldn't have a chance to settle anywhere. Forcing herself back on task, she peered inside the locker. "Janie, you were a packrat." Make-up bags, hair ties, hairbrushes, face wipes, lip balm, mints, even a book on baking from Hestia's Wholesome hits. "Why have a book from the competition?" Lila rummaged through Janie's life, but other than the competition's recipe book, everything seemed normal...

She took a step back and squinted at the locker. She opened the empty locker next to Janie's and compared the space in each. The empty locker seemed bigger. Granted, Janie had her life's overflow stashed in hers, but something still didn't add up. Lila tapped the back of the locker, her curiosity rewarded by a hollow thump. "False back, you sneaky bakery assistant. I'm impressed." Using her latex-covered fingers, Lila pried the back open. A plastic bag lay hidden behind the false back. Lila carefully drew the bag out and upended it gently onto the break room table. Two separated bags lay in front of her. "Spoiled for choices."

Lila picked up one baggie and drew the contents out. "An empty spell bottle, a hex bag for spoiling food, and a bag of dog food with sleepy-bye written on it." Janie had dog food to put Nash to sleep but hadn't used it. "Was that when you drew the line, Janie? Hurting Nash?" Lila muttered to herself, then turned to the other sealed bag. This was much more practical. "List of my suppliers, my delivery schedule for the last month and a mold for a key." Lila frowned. Why on earth would Janie need a mold unless she was making a copy of something? Lila picked up the mold, the shape pressed into it looked awfully like the key to Lila's apartment. "That's how the person who trashed my apartment got in. You made a copy of the key and gave it to them."

Lila dropped the mold, feeling violated. Janie hadn't deserved to die but having someone you trust connive and betray you behind your back was hard to forgive and forget. She picked up the last item in the bag, a small pocket notebook. As she did, a folded triangle of paper used as a bookmark fell out. Putting the notebook to the side, Lila unfolded the paper and gasped as she realized just what it meant. A pay slip for the Hestia Wholesome Hits company, dated two months before Janie started working at Lila's bakery.

"Hestia paid Janie to sabotage my bakery." Lila

sat back, shocked. She realized after the phone call that Janie was involved in something nefarious. But sabotaging her bakery? And the person who signed off on the pay slip? That horrible pushy Hestia rep, Marie Hestis. Lila picked up the notebook and flicked through, still shocked to see just how under-handed Janie had acted. The scribbled word *brownie* caught Lila's attention. Janie had jotted down ideas of ingredients that might be in Lila's Decadent Death by Brownie recipe.

"Those Hecate-cursed brownies. I wish I'd never made them."

"I wish you made more honey cake." Zach Braun, resplendent in his black Police Chief uniform, leaned against the door. "What have I told you about disturbing potential evidence?"

"Don't get caught?" Lila winced. Zach was a pretty good guy, and he mostly had the Harrow back. She hated pushing him to the brink of losing his temper. The poor man put up with a lot from the Harrow family.

"That's Elspeth." He strolled and sat next to Lila, snapping on his own latex gloves. "What do you have?"

"Janie worked for Hestia Wholesome Hits."

"The company trying to buy your recipes? I heard Grim had a run-in with the rep who's visiting."

"Yeah, that one. Apparently, Janie helped sabotage my bakery. Ruin food, hex the fridge, drop my cake mixes, my power going out. All Janie. She even copied my apartment key."

"The break-in? That could have ended badly for you, Lila. That's serious."

Lila slapped the table. "What's serious is that Janie tried to pull out of whatever scheme was planned next. I heard her on the phone this morning. She was refusing to work anymore for whoever's masterminding this dirty business."

"Did you confront her?" Zack frowned as he puzzled the pieces of the story together.

"Not really. I just let her know if she had trouble, I could help." Lila sniffed. "She told me she'd keep it in mind, and she'd turned over a new leaf. I believed her."

"And you think someone killed her for saying no?"

"That's just it. I don't know. Who on earth would kill for a brownie recipe? It's ridiculous." She thunked her head on the table and winced. Foreheads should never take on break tables. But the pain helped flash an idea into a head. "What if the ploy to get my recipes and the deaths were separate issues?"

Zack frowned. "What do you mean?"

"That obstinate Hestia rep hiring Janie to sabotage my bakery, and the Keres Daimons killing people in Point Muse. I think they're two separate situations." Lila thumped her chest. "The link is me and I run the bakery, while my father's the one who arrested the sisters. But I think it's a coincidence. The two situations are completely separate."

"You think the killing carried out by the Daimons and the sabotage organized by the rep are different? The only link is you, correct?"

"Exactly. Neither one knows about the other. Honestly, who would kill for baked goods?" Lila held up a hand. "Don't answer that. But I still think my idea carries weight. The crimes aren't connected, it's just a coincidence."

Braun gathered up the evidence. "I'll look into this at the station. Get more of an idea of your theory."

"Our bakery witch has a theory?" Grim strolled in, hands in the pockets of his jeans. He unabashedly looked around with interest.

"Move along, reaper. No souls to collect here." Lila painted the inquisitive man with an Elspeth stare made to make a man squirm. But the reaper was made of sterner stuff and just smirked.

"Lila thinks the sabotage of her bakery and the murders are separate. She thinks it's a coincidence and the only common denominator between the two crimes is herself."

Matthew frowned, his forehead furrowed over suddenly steely gray eyes. "It's a possibility. Could be the Daimons are taking advantage of the smoke-screen the sabotage causes. Plus, deaths related to your bakery helps them get back at your father." He nodded. "It works for me."

"Glad it meets with your approval," Lila sniped back.

"On that sarcastic note, I'm heading back to the station with this evidence, if you want to go over it with me?" Zach invited the reaper.

Lila cleared her throat. "Before you go, I have a couple of questions."

Zach nodded. "Shoot."

"When can I open?"

"Probably tomorrow if nothing else happens."

"Awesome." That was something she could look forward to. "Thanks, Zach. I appreciate it."

"And the second question?" Matthew cut in.

Lila licked her lips, unsure how to proceed.

"Janie. How did she? I mean…" She stuttered to a stop, unsure how to broach the subject of how her assistant died.

"How did she pass away?" Zach gently asked.

Lila nodded.

"Massive blunt force trauma due to crashing into the statue, plus the impact snapped her neck. I'm sorry, Lila, but if it's any consolation, it would've been fast."

Lila nodded her thanks. "Anything to add, reaper?"

"She had a cross incision on the back of her hand."

"When the accident happened, two women ran up to help straight away, before anyone else could react. Winifred told me the other women had run off to get help. But what if those women were actually the Keres sisters?"

Grin's jaw flexed. "You saw them? You need to stay away from those psychotic hags. They have an axe to grind with your father and wouldn't hesitate to hurt you to get back at him."

"It's not me you have to worry about. They *are* weird and stalkers. *And* turn up wherever I am, not the other way around. Besides…" Lila surged up and pointed her finger a scant distance away from

Matthew's nose. "You don't tell me what to do, reaper."

Grim batted her finger away. "I'm trying to keep you alive. You'll thank me in the future when you have a life to live. You're a trouble magnet, I swear."

"*Oh*." Lila reared back, hands to her chest. "You did not just call me Elspeth."

"On that inflammatory note, I'm leaving. Quickly." Braun gathered his evidence and backed out of the room, his gaze trained on the warring duo like they were dangerous animals ready to pounce.

"I said trouble magnet, not Elspeth. Maybe you need to listen more clearly."

Lila surged forward, pushed her face as close to the reaper's as she could and jutted her chin out. "You don't get away with calling me an Elspeth clone. That crosses a line. Besides, I'm not the one whose daddy had to come and check up on."

Matthew secured Lila's hand between his and glared down at the witchy baker. "My Dad's concerned because Point Muse has a murder issue. Bodies keep turning up, as do the Harrows."

Lila tried to take her hand away, but Matthew's grip tightened. His warm hand short-circuited her thoughts and temper. "The Harrows would never... I don't..." She stumbled to a stop, staring up into gray eyes that resembled fluffy clouds instead of his normal steely hard gaze.

His grip softened and he stroked a thumb over the soft skin of Lila's hand. "I don't want you hurt and you seem to be caught up in the center of everything."

"Not by design." Every time the sneaky reaper's thumb moved across the skin of her hand it shorted out her brain processes. Words forgotten, they stared at each other.

A hellhound tornado burst into the room and made a beeline for Lila. With a mini growl, Nash forced his way between the two adults, shoving them apart.

Lila reared back against the table and shook her head to dispel the foggy feeling in her brain.

Grim cleared his throat. "Stay out of trouble. That's all I ask. And if you're interested, my dad is with your grandmother. I'd be more worried about that than sticking my nose into a murder investigation." The reaper ignored Lila and stomped out of the room.

"If that's your seduction technique, it needs work. I'm not impressed," Lila bellowed. As a comeback, it sucked, but when your brain operated on limited power, bakers couldn't be choosers. Lila scratched Nash's soft ears. "Thanks buddy. You just saved me from a fate worse than running out of sugar." Lusting after the reaper equaled Lila Stooped-Head living in a world of Elspeth match-making regret. Lila was a lone baker, not a reaper groupie.

Now if she could just convince herself of that...

SIXTEEN

"Gas leak. That's all I can think of to write off my momentary dazed condition. A gas leak situated only in my break room that affected my brain functions." Lila nodded and iced another cupcake. "It's the simplest answer. Occam's razor and all that."

"So, you're going with a gas leak in the break room because the simplest answer is the right one?"

"Exactly. What else could it be?"

"You're attracted to him, and you were both having a moment?" Xandie arched an eyebrow at her cousin in denial.

"No. Absolutely not." Lila pointed a cupcake at her cousin, shaking the baked good for emphasis. "I'm not like you and Braun. Fighting and flirting is not our thing. And I definitely did *not* stay up all night stressing over what happened in the break room yesterday."

"Aha," Xandie crowed. "You and the reaper are a thing. I knew it. Holly owes me ten dollars. Score."

Lila glared. "I hate how Harrows bet on family issues. It's demeaning."

"And how much cash did you make on Zach and me?"

"That's beside the point." Lila waved Xandie's words away.

"Another point is why you're baking for the reaper if you don't like him?"

"I..." Lila paused in the middle of placing cupcakes in a plastic container. "I'm bribing him into a good mood, so he'll stay out of my way when I track those Keres sisters down. That's what." Lila slammed the lid closed on the container.

"I stand corrected. It's all about the murder, not how good you think he looks in tight jeans. "

"Exactly." Lila nodded, then looked confused. "I think so. Um, I don't think I mentioned what he looks like in jeans?"

Xandie hid her snicker behind a cupcake. "I hear the nosy Grim stomping down the stairs. You might want to catch him before he heads out. Otherwise, your bribery plan is a bust."

"You're right." Snatching up her container, Lila hotfooted it from the kitchen to the stairs that led up to her apartment, surprising the reaper as he opened the door separating the stairs from the bakery.

"Whoops. Sorry." Lila stepped out of the way.

"No worries." Matthew shuffled from foot to foot. "I have to head out for a while. I've organized an interview with a potential witness. I'll text Braun with the details."

"Okay." Lila mentally slapped herself in the head. How awkward and painful did they sound? If it'd been Xandie talking, she'd have laughed a lung up. Lila shoved her cupcakes at him. "Here, take these. Might loosen up the witness's tongue."

"Cupcakes?"

"I say sorry with sugar. I don't know what came over me yesterday in the break room. I blame a gas leak."

"A gas leak?" Grim nodded. "You get leaks in your break room often?"

"It's Point Muse. You'd be surprised." Lila shoved the container at Matthew's hard chest. "Take it."

He gripped the container tight. "Thanks. I accept your sugar apology." He paused. "You could do me a favor, though."

"Sure."

"I'm expecting a call from work. I have someone exploring a lead outside of Point Muse today. Can you tell them I'm on an interview and I'll update them later? I'll be back within an hour. Dad's off with Elspeth somewhere if you have any issues."

"I can do that, and I'll be fine." Lila forced a smile and nodded to Matthew as he left.

"I understand why you used to choke on your spit when you watched Braun and me. That was especially awkward."

Lila spun, glaring at her cousin. "No comments from the peanut gallery. Now scoot. Don't you have books to shelve?"

"One or two. But first I have to detour past Harrow house for a gossip update. Tata." Xandie smirked evilly and sauntered out.

"Everyone's a comedian when it comes to my non-existent love life."

"And then again, some of us just don't care." A tall, skinny young woman in her twenties, with long black hair, stood framed in the door of the bakery.

"I keep forgetting to lock that door," Lila muttered. She plastered a professional smile in place. "I'm afraid we aren't open today. You could try tomorrow."

"I'm not after cupcakes. Yours seem cursed anyway. Just want to pop in, say hi and see how you're going. See if any murderous killers managed to off you yet."

"Do we know each other?" Lila eyed the young woman. An eye-bleaching combination of a tight purple flowered shirt, a bright yellow leather skirt paired with orange boots may have befuddled her mind somewhat. But there was something familiar about the girl.

The woman strutted in and trailed her baby pink painted talons over a table. "Such a disappointment, a smart witch like you doesn't take after her father. Now that Shade is clued in."

"Lys." She'd recognize that smart mouth anywhere.

"Ding, ding, ding. We have a winner." The Daimon cackled and stalked around Lila. "Honestly, I can really see the attraction of Point Muse. This town does have some murderous undercurrents." Lys inhaled and let her breath out with a happy smile. "Delicious."

"The police are looking for you and I have an employee out back who's probably ringing the Chief right now. Plus, the reaper upstairs." Lila lied about

Matthew without a blink or a twitch. Maybe she took after Elspeth after all.

"Really?" Lys sneered then let out a cackle worthy of Elspeth. "The capacity for subterfuge by humans is truly inspiring. In other words, sweet pea, the Brownie's obsessed with the magazine I conveniently left in your kitchen and the reaper left." Lys winked. "Just us girls."

"You mean girl and hag Daimon."

"Potato, potahto. Whatever the saying is, let's get down to business." Lys planted her yellow-leather-clad booty on a chair. "Enter the neutral zone, and let's have a discussion."

"I knew I should have brought my Taser to work today."

Lys ignored Lila's comments and continued, "We have a genuine grievance with your father." The Daimon leaned forward, palms flat on the table. "I'll be honest, your sugary sweetness plagues me, but Ana likes you. How about we make a deal?"

"Have you met my grandmother? Sugary sweet does not make up the core of the Harrow women. And didn't you already have a deal with Hades that you broke?"

"That baldheaded tyrant wouldn't know a deal if it tore his heart out and ate it."

"That's an oddly specific and gruesome image." And Lila had no doubt the hags would delight in ripping the God's heart out given the chance. "I don't think I'm authorized to negotiate for the entire underworld. Bakers don't normally deal with vengeful death spirits."

Lys stood so abruptly her chair fell on its side. She hissed at Lila, "So judgmental. I tried to do you a good deal, Harrow. But you're obviously not ready to admit you need our help."

What whacked-out sugar trip was this hag on? "You're killing people, I don't think that's helping me."

"None so blind as those that don't see. Watch your step, Harrow. Because we'll be watching and waiting."

The kitchen door swung open, and Nash bounded in. The hellhound had swollen to the size of a small pony. Red flames flickered to life in his eyes and smoke trickled out of his nose.

Lys screeched and flung some tables and chairs in the hellhound's path.

Ignoring the furniture, Nash, leaped forward, his nails gouging burned furrows into Lila's floor. He reared back and belched out a blast of flames and heat, along with the smell of vanilla cupcakes. The aroma spread through the bakery.

Lys bolted for the door, the bottom of her long black hair smoking. She flung the door open and surged outside.

Nash galloped to the door and huffed proudly. He shrunk to his normal large puppy size. His fiery red eyes flickered back to brown. He quirked his head, considering Lila.

Sighing, she contemplated her semi-destroyed bakery. At least all the fire disappeared when Nash shrunk back to normal size.

"I heard the snip controls a dog's aggressive behavior." Hester shrugged. "Then again, with a number of enemies you're garnering, maybe you need a little aggression around you."

"Bill Hades. We can always offer a pop-up store out front while the repairs are completed."

"Who are you, pod person, and what have you done with our Lila?"

"Maybe I need to roll with the cookie dough? I'm getting a headache with all the threats I've received lately." Lila rubbed the aforementioned head. Honestly, she didn't know how Xandie coped with the tension of all the unanswered questions. Why would Lys want to make a deal? They were having the time of their lives slicing and dicing in Point

Muse. Why warn her instead of just killing her? Two questions and not enough answers. The peal of the bakery phone rang through the bakery.

Lila waved off Hester. "That's probably Grim's work. I'll get it and take a message."

Hester nodded and disappeared back into the kitchen.

Nash, exhausted from his demonic showdown, lay spread-eagled on the floor under a table, snoring.

"So much for my great protector now," Lila grumbled half-heartedly. He had stepped in to warn Lys off. She probably shouldn't be so hard on him. Reaching for the phone, Lila lifted the handset. "Heart's Delight Bakery, Lila Harrow speaking."

"Would that be the Lila Harrow renting an apartment to my son and his freeloading father?" A warm female voice flowed down the line.

"That would be me. Or at least my grandmother's renting the apartment. Matthew told me to expect a call from his work. Something about a lead outside Point Muse?"

"I'm his long-suffering mother, Isabel Grim. But you can call me Izzy. I've heard a lot about you, Lila."

"Probably all bad and mostly true. I am a Harrow after all." Lila shrugged. Matthew's mother sounded too nice to put up with the Grim men.

"Why, thank you, dear. Agree with you."

Oops, Lila may have spoken that last sentence out loud.

A rich chuckle vibrated in Lila's ear.

"Sorry, there's not much of a filter with the Harrows," Lila plunged on, trying not to think about the poor impression she was making on Matthew's mother. "Matthew had to go out. He'll be back in under an hour. I can update him then."

"Typical, never around when you want to speak to him. He gets that from his father." Izzy sighed. "Lila, I hear you're an amazing baker. Matthew raves about your cupcakes."

Lila coughed as she swallowed spit. "Really? I got the impression he didn't like me much. He thought I was a cupcake-suffocating killer when we first met."

"A small misunderstanding. Matthew's the more sensitive of my brood. He worries, needs a solid grounded loving woman to take him in hand. My interfering husband mentioned you were single?"

Unholy matchmaking mothers. Lila cleared her throat. "I am, but my family has a certain reputation in Point Muse, especially with males. We don't have the best luck in relationships."

Izzy snorted delicately. "The Grim family

harvest souls to transport to the afterlife. We have a certain reputation too. You aren't seeing anyone, correct?"

Lila backpedaled. Matthew's mother was more single-minded about matchmaking than Elspeth and her aunts combined. "You need to discuss the subject with Matthew. He'll be back within the hour."

"Of course, dear. If you have any issues, just call Edwin's phone. His phone is spelled so he has to answer it, no matter what. Otherwise, he dodges my calls." Matthew's mother reeled off a line of numbers.

Lila scrambled to scribble the number on a notepad. "Thank you, Mrs. Grim."

"Izzy, don't forget. Nice talking to you, Lila. I'm sure I'll meet you soon."

With that ominous threat ringing in Lila's ears, Matthew's mother hung up.

Lila let out the breath she had no clue she'd been holding. "Wonder if Matthew realizes his mother is on the hunt for a girlfriend for him?" Shaking her head, she wandered off to the kitchen and joined Hester in cleaning every available surface of the bakery.

"Trouble?" Hester enquired.

"A matchmaking mother, trying to encourage me to date her youngest, emotional Grim son."

"Matthew Grim's emotional and can't get a date?" Hester cast a horrified look at Lila before she broke into hysterical laughter.

Getting a breath, Lila leaned against the counter. "Mother's little boy is the apple of her eye. Somehow, I think Matthew would be horrified if he'd heard that phone call." Speaking of Matthew... Lila checked her watch. Just over an hour had passed since he'd left.

"Problem?"

"Grim said he'd be an hour. It's an hour now."

"The interview went longer than expected." Hester shrugged. "Any idea who the meeting was with and where?"

"No clue. He never mentioned it. I'll give him another hour and then start worrying." Lila pointed at the cleaning cupboard. "Meanwhile, it's mopping time."

Lila grabbed cleaning products as Hester wielded the mop. *Grim was an adult, a reaper. Nothing to worry about.* So why did her stomach churn like she'd swallowed one of Elspeth's weird cocktail concoctions? Lila shook off the worry and immersed herself in stripping the germs from her beloved bakery.

A few hours later, Lila straightened with a groan. "My back. I hate cleaning. Isn't there some sort of witch or Brownie spell that would do it for us?"

"Stop your whining. Hard labor builds character."

"Certainly builds blisters," Lila grumbled at Hester and checked her watch. "That's it. Grim has a protective streak a mile wide. There's no way he would leave me alone for over two hours. Something's wrong." Lila dug out the number Izzy Grim had given her and punched it into a phone. She listened to the phone ring before a click heralded somebody picking up.

"Izzy. I gave you all the information I had on the girl. If you want to set up a date, call her and organize it."

"She already did and gave me your number in case of trouble. And that's what we've got."

"Lila?"

Ed's confused voice sounded loud in Lila's ears.

"Matthew went out almost three hours ago for an interview and hasn't come back. I've already had a visit from one Keres sister this morning, while the other one was conspicuously absent. I think they may have Matthew."

"Reapers' balls," Ed cursed. "I'll contact Braun and try to get a magical trace on Matthew. Stay there. Lock the shop up. I'll send some troops to protect you."

"I don't need..." Lila listened to the dial tone and hung up, "...any protection from the troops, whoever they are."

Matthew needed protection more than she did...

SEVENTEEN

"When he said he'd send in the troops, I kinda thought it would be other hunky Grim reapers," Lila whined to her cousins.

Holly nodded glumly. "I'd take the reapers any day."

Xandie slapped Lila's back. "Cheer up. You get your grandmother, her mouthy dog, and your favorite Police Chief instead. "

"Yippee."

"It could be worse." Xandie paused dramatically. "Your mother could have come too."

Lila shuddered. "From your lips to Hades' ears. Seriously, normally she'd jump at a chance to over-protect me. Don't tell me she's been kidnapped as well?"

Elspeth flounced into the kitchen, Colin under one arm, her emerald curly wig clashing with her orange jogging suit. "We should be so lucky. She and your sperm donor headed off for quiet time this morning, before the ruckus started." Elspeth rolled her eyes. "In my day we called it like it was. Nookie, bumping uglies, cherry time..."

Lila gagged and held up a hand. "Stop. The images are seared into my brain. Permanent scarring."

"You and me both, kid." Colin the pug wiggled until Elspeth placed him down on the floor. He nosed around until he found a patch of late after-noon sun on the floor next to a sleeping Nash. "I have nightmares too. About your mom's vet clinic. That dame threatens me daily with the loss of my manhood. She's vicious." Colin shuddered and everyone in the room covered their noses just in case.

"Wusses." Elspeth settled herself on a stool. "Now, what's our game plan? Do we have proof of life yet?"

"I have no clue what that means, but I'd feel way more comfortable if Xandie's mother was here. She at least has black ops training." Xandie had thought her mother died over twenty years ago when a killer Knight had forced Miranda over a cliff. But she'd survived with amnesia, thanks to a human only, black ops division of the government. Eventually, she'd recovered her memories, took down her employers and reconnected with the family again.

"Mom's visiting Dad in Andrews again. She'll come if necessary, but I prefer not to contact her yet." Xandie shrugged. "She and Dad are getting along really well. I don't want to rock the boat."

Elspeth tapped the island bench with a fuchsia-colored, hex-painted nail. "Hello, Miranda isn't the only one with black ops training. I have mad killing skills."

"I'm going to forget I ever heard that." Braun entered the kitchen.

Lila stood as Braun crossed to Xandie and drifted a gentle kiss across her nose. Lila bit her lip. Until now, she'd always been happy with her single status. Thanks to a nosy reaper, she'd started to think that Xandie and Braun had the right idea. Fight, flirt, and kiss and make up. She just had to track down one disappearing reaper first. "Did you find anything?"

"No. I sent Ed out to canvas around town and I need Elspeth to head down to the harbor and nose around. I have my deputies searching the rest of the town and the outlying areas. We'll find him, Lila. I promise."

Lila sniffed in pretend disinterest. At least for now. "What do you need Xandie, Holly and me to do?"

"Stay here."

"What?" Lila stamped her foot, casual disinterest all but forgotten. "You need us. Why bench your best players?"

"This is not a sport, and the Keres sisters still pose a threat to you. Plus, if Grim makes it back here, I need to know." Braun narrowed his gaze on Lila. "Do you understand me, Lila Marie Harrow?"

"I heard you, bear." Lila deflated and collapsed onto a stool next to Elspeth, who patted her hand.

"Never mind, girl. Your reaper love bunny will be back in your sugary claws quicker than a soufflé can rise."

Lila drew her hand away, avoiding her grandmother's hex-painted nails, and any stray electricity that was hanging around her knuckles. "Can you not do love and food analogies? It creeps me out."

"It's your grandfather's do-gooder genes, it washes the gumption out of every generation." Elspeth hopped off the stool and gathered Colin onto a hip again. "Right, I'm off to the harbor. I'll radio in if I find him." Elspeth stomped off.

Braun gave Xandie a quick squeeze. "I need to

coordinate with Caleb and Riley. I'll call you later." He winked at Xandie and left.

"Right, now they've gone, dig in." Hester dumped a tray of hot savory biscuits on the island bench and bustled around, fixing hot chocolate and sweet tea.

Nabbing a hot biscuit, Lila blew on it before munching away. Matthew had been missing for hours. Sunset wasn't far away now. Lila thumped her chest as the biscuit and a mysterious hard lump refused to go down. She reached for the sweet tea Hester had just placed in front of her and swallowed hurriedly.

"You okay?" Holly nudged Lila's shoulder.

"Why does everyone keep asking me that? Grim thought I was a killer of cupcake lovers. Why should I care if he's missing?"

"Because he's grown on you, and he's decided he likes fiery bakery witches." Xandie savored Hester's hot chocolate with a little sigh.

Hester winked and bustled off into the bakery, leaving the cousins and Nash alone in the kitchen.

"There's no one else here. You might as well admit our mouthy drama llama Lila has a thing for the dude who packs a stick."

"Holly," Xandie gasped out a chuckle.

"A scythe, not a stick." Lila rolled her eyes. "Fine. I will admit he's not as bad as I thought and doesn't deserve to be kidnapped by killer Daimon hags on a revenge trip. But that's it. *Got it.*" Lila glared at her cousins, unwilling to admit out loud her interest in the reaper.

Hester poked her head into the kitchen. "You girls need to get to the Inn, ASAP. There's been some kind of ruckus upstairs. Rose wants Lila at the Inn, seems to think it's something to do with your missing guy."

"About time a lead reared up and slapped me in the face." Lila jumped up and kicked her heels like Dorothy from the Wizard of Oz. "Xandie, go find Braun. Let him know where we are, and I'll head to the Inn on Holly's deathtrap."

Holly frowned. "My moped is perfectly safe."

"I call them as I see them. Hester," Lila bellowed. "Look after Nash for me." She dragged Holly out the bakery door and into the alley.

Whatever Rose had going on at the Inn, hopefully, it'd lead her to her annoying reaper before his whole family arrived en masse in Point Muse.

"I swear. I should move from Point Muse. No one gives me the respect a descendant of Aphrodite is due."

"Point Muse would definitely be quieter," Lila murmured to Holly, catching Rose's beady eye. "What can we help you with?"

Rose shot a panicked look around before shoving a set of keys into Lila's hands. "This is my master set of keys. It will let you into any room in the Inn. I need you to deal with the issue and for the love of Aphrodite, keep quiet."

Holly smiled encouragingly at Rose. "Of course, we will. But you haven't told us the issue yet?"

"Oh." Rose appeared flustered for a moment. "Those two weird women from the bar were upstairs causing a ruckus with another paying customer. Raised voices, glass breaking. I won't have it, Harrows. Do you hear me?"

"Did you check it out?"

"Do I look like Nancy Drew or security to you, Lila Harrow?"

"That would be a negative, Rose. You said it's connected to the Harrows? How?" Lila prodded the Inn owner.

"That man you're living with spoke to the paying guest just before those two freaky women caused a fight. Clean the mess up and get those women out of my Inn. Room twelve." Rose glared at the cousins and pointed upstairs.

Ignoring Rose, Lila took the stairs two a time.

"Whoa, someone's upped their cardio or sugar intake. Slow down," Holly puffed behind Lila.

"Nope. This is the first lead we've managed to dig up on Matthew's whereabouts. I'm not letting it slip through my fingers."

"It, or him, slipped through your fingers?" Holly teased her cousin.

Lila counted the doors as she moved along the hallway. "I'm ignoring you. Room twelve." Lila used the master keys and unlocked the door. She edged it open and peered through the exposed gap. Nothing moved, no noises. Taking a risk, Lila opened the door and stepped in, Holly crowding behind her.

"Looks like Grim had a wild party." Holly winced as she tiptoed through a minefield of broken teacups. "How do we even know he was here? Rose isn't exactly known as the font of all truth."

Lila fished an empty Tupperware container out of the mess and held it up. "Because I gave this to Grim as he left for the interview. He was definitely here." *Annoying reaper.* "Trust Matthew to interview a witness and get himself kidnapped along with my cupcakes."

"You think the sisters kidnapped him?"

"Who else?" Lila pointed to an overturned table, squished food, and broken teacups. "Yep, and probably the guest he interviewed as well. Do we know who rented the room?"

Holly held up a handful of Hestia Wholesome Hits business cards. "About that? I think your favorite pushy rep rented the room."

Lila groaned. "That woman is the bane of my baking life."

Without warning, the door to the room swung open and slammed against the wall. Lila and Holly screeched as Edwin Grim stood framed in the doorway, massive arms crossed over his chest.

"Where's my son?"

Putting a hand to her racing heart, Lila took a few stabilizing breaths. "Am I too young to have a heart attack? Because it feels like one."

Ed stepped into the room. "Baker, do you know where my little boy is?"

Lila shook her head. "No clue, but we think he and Marie Hestis, who rented this room, were kidnapped by the Keres sisters."

"Typical death spirits. All about revenge." Ed

rubbed his hands. "Right, I'll hook up with Braun. Let them know we have proof of the kidnapping. You two need to head back to the bakery or Harrow House and hunker down." Ed held the door open, waiting for the girls to walk through.

"How come Elspeth gets to join the hunt and we're sent back to the bakery with a pat on the head?" Lila grouched at Matthew's father. "Women's liberation and all that."

Ed held his hands up. "Don't look at me. I'm just passing on Elspeth's orders. It's your funeral if you want to disregard her instructions." The elder reaper shuddered. "I wouldn't recommend it, though. She's nasty when riled."

"You have no idea. Try living with her." Holly snagged Lila and drew her to a stop. "We'll head right back to the bakery, Mr. Grim, and wait for news." She smiled sweetly as he walked past and patted her shoulder.

"Good girl. Always do what Elspeth says." Ed nodded to the duo and headed downstairs.

"You're a good girl, Holly. Blah, blah, suck up," Lila snarked. Xandie, the bookworm, Holly the good girl, and Lila the drama llama. She definitely got the rough end of the Harrow DNA.

"Ever thought there might be a reason for my sweet smile? I *am* a Harrow."

"Nope. You're just a suck-up."

Holly whacked Lila on the arm. "Thanks a lot. Let Ed think we're going back to the bakery while we hunt around for more clues. There has to be something else that might help track him down."

Lila smiled slowly and linked arms with her cousin. "I think I'll keep you."

The cousins sauntered downstairs and paused at reception.

"Is it all sorted out?" Rose hissed as she kept her head down, pretending to ignore the Harrows.

Lila dumped the keys on the desk. "No one's there, but the room is trashed. Looks like the reaper and your guest were kidnapped by the weird sisters."

"Aphrodite's unburdened loins," Rose cursed. "Who's going to pay for the damage now?"

"Bill Hestia Wholesome Hits." Lila strolled out, Holly trailing behind.

"Where do we look?"

"You take the bar, Holly. I'll pick outside. Meet me there when you're finished." Slipping out, Lila paced around the Inn, but nothing seemed disturbed. Using light shining from the windows to see, she scanned the area. *No neon signs blinking a clue here.*

A cool wind blew in and Lila shivered. Matthew had been missing for hours. Surely there had to be something pointing to where he'd gone?

A scuffle behind her was Lila's only warning as she spotted two dark shadows in her peripheral vision. Ducking down behind a prickly bush, she concentrated on the shadows and their hushed whispers.

"Where's the meet?"

"Out back of the funeral home. Of course."

"Appropriate."

The accompanying cackle clued Lila into just who she spied on. Ana and Lys Keres, the Daimons, but there was no trace of a kidnapped reaper or the pushy Hestia rep.

"Everything set?"

"The final pieces are now in play."

"Let's get moving."

The two figures blended back into the shadows and disappeared.

"Sniffing that bush?" Holly stood next to Lila and stared at her cousin and the straggly bush she hid behind.

Lila stood and dusted off her jeans. "Forget the bush. I think I know where Grim is."

"You psychic?"

"No. I'm an eavesdropper. Just heard the hags talking about a meet out the back of the funeral home."

"And our mothers always said snooping would never get us anywhere." Holly giggled.

"Get back inside and call Grim senior. Tell him Matthew's at the funeral home."

"What about you?"

Lila beamed at her cousin. "I'm about to take a crash course in driving a moped, then take a tour of a funeral home."

Hopefully not a permanent one...

EIGHTEEN

"Elysian Fields is zombie free. Elysian Fields is zombie free," Lila chanted as she crouched behind a headstone in the cemetery.

"Horror movie waiting to happen and I'm TSTL." Too stupid to live. Who goes into a cemetery at night to rescue a reaper? How did Holly work here on a daily basis? Lila shivered. Give her a well-lit, non-dead-person bakery any day.

"Speaking of Holly's work..." Where were her twin creepy bosses? Surely if a duo of death spirits and a couple of kidnap victims were hanging around the funeral home, the necromancers would spot them?

Unwilling to remain hiding behind a headstone, Lila scooted from shadow to shadow and made her way to the funeral home. Since she had Holly's moped, she had her cousin's work keys as well. Lila fiddled with the keyring until she found the old spindly one that fit into a small old-fashioned, wooden door built into the side of the home. Holly had shown her the door ages ago in case of trouble. This situation classified as trouble. Opening the door, Lila scuttled in, closing it quickly behind her. The old-fashioned door opened into a small storage area. The necromancers used the biggest storage room around the back now, so this room stood mostly unused, judging from the number of cobwebs.

Lila swiped at the back of her neck and shivered. Spiders and cobwebs didn't form part of her happy place, but they were better than soul-sucking death hags out for revenge against their captor's family. Avoiding the cobwebs, Lila scooted to the door and inched it open. All the lights were off except for tiny little nightlights which twinkled like fairy lights at the base of the wall. "Necromancers afraid of the dark? Now I've seen everything."

Now if I were an evil hag, where would I store freaky necromancers if I wanted them out of the way? Lila tried a few door handles as she moved along the hallway, but each room was locked up tight. The hair lifted on Lila's arms and the back of her neck as she crept along the darkened hallway. Even with the pretty little nightlights, way too many shadows and dark corners loomed for Lila's sense of well-being. She pressed her elbows into her side, making her body as small a target as possible. There were only a few doors left in this portion of the funeral home. The slab room and the viewing room. The slab room was as titled—a room with slabs for bodies to be worked on by the necromancers in preparation for burial. Lila licked her lips. She'd leave that until last.

"Viewing room, it is." At least she'd been there before, when Holly and Hector had raved over some new coffin. The viewing room stood in its own little alcove. Two entrances, one for the public and one for employees.

Lila opened the employees' door very slowly. Again, the room seemed deserted, but at least low lights illuminated the interior instead of creepy shadows. Lila crept in and paused. The room had rich velvet couches and small tables dotted here and there, but nowhere to hide, except for...three closed coffins on stands.

"Ah man. I need danger pay," Lila whimpered, but still stepped to the nearest coffin. She raised trembling hands and gripped the coffin's lid, knuckles white. With a grunt, she raised it then sagged in relief as the contents registered as empty. Bad news, she'd have to do this all over again, *twice.* "Come on, Lila. Steel spine and a steady hand." She moved to the next coffin. Sweat beaded on her top lip and Lila wiped a clammy hand over it. Taking a deep breath, she gripped the coffin lid again and yanked the lid up. Lila eased one eye open and then both as the bound and gagged figure of Hector, Holly's boss, met her creeped-out gaze. "Bingo." Lila clutched the duct tape and ripped it off Hector's mouth in one smooth move.

Hector drew a breath in. "Thank Hades. I thought no one would find us in time." He knocked the side of the coffin with an elbow. "These things are built for the dead. Although the padding is surprisingly comfortable. With a few adjustments..."

"No offence, but I need to untie you and ungag your sister before she suffocates." Lila worked on the edge of the tape securing his hands. Finally tearing an edge, she managed to unwind the tape. She patted Hector on his lace-covered chest. "Upsy daisy." Lila grabbed the necromancer's arm and helped support him as he clambered out of his not-so-final resting place. She dusted him off and pointed him in the direction of the third coffin. "I'm in a bit of a time crunch. You'll have to let your sister out."

"Of course." He hurried to open the other coffin and rip the tape off his sister's mouth.

"Hades' fanged freaks. It's about time. I nearly asphyxiated hearing you ramble about the coffin's bedding," Hillary snarled.

"Can I put the tape back on?" her brother muttered.

"No time to bicker. I have two kidnapping victims to rescue and Daimon hags to stop."

"What?"

"That's not..."

The two necromancers' protests collided. Lila held a hand up. "Whoa there, take a breath. You guys need to get out of here, the cops hopefully are already on their way. But right now, I need to find my reaper." Lila stuttered to a stop, then tried again. "I mean, *the* reaper." With a wave, Lila ducked out into the hallway, ignoring the muttering behind her. She moved back down the hallway and into the disused storage room. She edged the door open and slipped out, flattening herself against the wall outside.

She blinked her eyes furiously. Even though the lights inside were only nightlights, she still needed time to adjust to outside night vision. Meanwhile, she strained her ears for any audible clues as to the hags' whereabouts. After a few minutes, her eyes adapted enough she could make out the headstones and other shadows in the graveyard. All those beautiful angel statues spread throughout the cemetery now looked like potential demonic villains. A rustle near some bushes to the left had Lila hyperfocused. She crept along the side of the funeral home in the direction of the noise. Lila's stomach cramped and she blew out a silent breath. She should've grabbed some kind of weapon from inside the funeral home.

The bushes rustled again, accompanied this time by a low growl. A ferocious growl. A growl that sounded familiar. "Nash." Lila pounced on the shrub and uncovered a red-eyed, but not yet humongous-sized hellhound puppy. His red eyes remained but now Nash panted and licked Lila's hand.

"I'm glad to see you, boy. The cemetery is *not* my go-to place for fun," Lila whispered to the puppy and gave him a quick squeeze. As she did so, something sharp pricked her hand. "What do you have there?"

Lila drew out a pencil-size, sharply pointed reaper scythe. "How did you get hold of Matthew's stick thingy?"

Nash pranced on the spot, proud of himself.

"Can you show me where you found Matthew's

scythe? Good puppy." Lila blew an air kiss at her hellhound.

Nash shook himself and bounded toward the back of the cemetery land. Following his red eyes, Lila cursed herself that she hadn't thought to bring a flashlight. She gripped the reaper scythe tight. Matthew would never let his stick thingy out of sight, except if he was hurt. Or maybe he knew Nash would find a way to give it to Lila. She rubbed the side of her face and tried swallowing around a dry mouth. She should have waited for Braun and Matthew's father, but the less time the kidnapped spent with the Daimons, the better.

Nash stopped near the edge of the property where a large clump of shadowed trees stood.

"Good boy," Lila whispered to Nash.

Instead of prancing with pride, the puppy swung around, his hackles sticking straight up.

Lila jerked around to face the threat Nash had already spotted.

"Like taking sugar from a baker," Lys cackled and swiped a clawed hand over Lila's head.

Ducking and scooting back, Lila shoved the reaper scythe into her jeans pocket. She had no clue how to use it and would probably break it anyway, so hidden away it was.

"I think the human phrase is like taking candy from a baby." Ana kicked out at Lila, taking her to the ground. "So sorry, Lila, dear. But needs must."

"Back off, hag." Lila scooted until she ended up with her back against a tree. She scrabbled around on the ground and came up with a sturdy tree limb. She sprang upright and brandished her woody weapon. "My needs are gonna kick your dead booty."

The two death spirits converged on Lila, talons extended, hair flying behind them, and sharp teeth exposed.

Nash pounced in front of Lila, his eyes glaring and searing flames, his size now that of a small pony. A growl echoed out of the hellhound, forming into intelligible words for the first time. "Not hurt my pet." On the last word, he bared his fangs and leapt at the hags.

"Now you talk?" Lila registered his words. "I'm not a pet," she yelled indignantly. "You are."

The hags screeched, cowering until Lys blew a handful of dirt into Nash's eyes, blinding him momentarily. "Grave dirt has many uses. Quick, sister."

Anna flicked out a honey-colored rope that wrapped around Nash. "Sorry, puppy. But this is a rope blessed by Hecate herself. No chewing your way out and interfering with our plans."

Nash belched a searing, blood-red flame at the Daimon which she dodged.

"Naughty, naughty." Ana waggled her finger at the puppy.

"Leave my hound alone, hag." Lila rushed Ana with a branch, screeching like a wild woman. She jabbed her woody weapon at the hag's eyes.

Ana bent over, screeching. "My eyes, my eyes."

"Victory," Lila whooped and hoisted her branch into the air.

"Not so much." Lys bought a hand down on the back of Lila's head, ending the victory cry.

Lila crumpled to the ground; her wooden war stick discarded in her collapse. Thumping drums played a beat in her head, and she closed her eyes for a second before forcing them open.

Ana straightened and shot a murderous glance at Lila. "To think I liked you. I'm going to have to re-stick my eyelash extensions back on now." Moaning, Ana pulled off the fake eyelashes. "Farewell, human grooming magic. You made my eyes pop." Anna lowered her head piously as she spoke and threw the fake eyelashes into the air.

"Seriously? You're the death spirits feared by

all." Lila pushed the pain away and attempted to stand. Nash, still bound, whimpered. "It's okay, puppy. We'll work out a way to escape," Lila soothed her hellhound.

"Not this time." Lys grabbed Lila by the arm and wrenched her up. "We have somewhere to be and a deal to be done. Just remember that. *We need a deal.*"

Ana winked at Lila, her eyelash ire forgotten. "Always have an iron in the forge and a backup plan."

"Keep your ears and eyes open, Harrow. You'll stay out of trouble that way." Lys jerked Lila forward. "We got somewhere today."

And so did she. Wherever the devious hags took her, Matthew Grimm was sure to be nearby.

Time for this baker girl to ride in and save the day and the reaper. If she could just get rid of the vengeful death hags, life would be so much easier.

NINETEEN

"Well, well. How the high and mighty Harrow has fallen."

"Lila, get outta here." A groggy Matthew tried standing, only to collapse at his kidnapper's feet.

The kidnapper shoved out a blue-shod heel and jabbed it into the reaper's back. "Quiet, you. I've got plans for that baker and it doesn't include her running away."

Lila shook her head. "Immortal death spirits make deals with obsessed baked goods employees?"

"I am not just a baked good employee," Marie Hestis, clad in a sky-blue business suit consisting of jacket and skirt, shrieked at Lila. "I am a descendant of Hestia, Goddess of Hearth and Home. Firstborn child of the titans, Kronos, and Rhea. You *will* give me respect."

Respect? The Hestia Wholesome Hits company rep might've started out immaculate in her high-powered business suit, but now rips covered the jacket, dirt had spread across her skirt and the woman's silver up-swept hairdo stood at an odd angle reminiscent of the leaning Tower of Pisa.

"Wasn't she supposed to be a virgin Goddess?"

"Don't you badmouth my great-great whatever grandmother." Marie foamed at the mouth, spit flying every which way.

Ana drew back, a horrified expression on her face.

Lys sighed. "Can we get to the deal before you lose your grip on sanity?"

Ana placed a light hand on Lila's shoulder and Lys stood close by.

Why did it suddenly seem as if the hags were protecting her, not selling her off to the psychotic demigod in a stained business suit?

"Fine. You give me the baker and I'll give you the reaper. Win-win situation."

Why on earth would the sisters want the reaper? "Is this mess all about my brownie recipe?" If she kept the sugar psycho villain-monologuing it might give them more time for the rescue party to reach them.

"Everything is about that recipe. It's my ticket to upper administration." Marie yanked at her falling tower of hair. "You don't know what it's like trying to live up to family expectations. Hestia is cool, calm, not driven by emotion. Succeeds at everything. If you don't make a name for yourself, you're out of the family business. Exiled. I can't have that. I need your recipe."

Grim moaned and rolled over onto all fours. "Grims don't negotiate."

Marie kicked the reaper in the chest. He collapsed back to the ground, retching. "Good thing I'm not dealing with you," Marie smirked.

"Not hurt man." Nash galloped in and launched himself at Marie, accidentally taking down the hags and Lila at the same time.

Marie dropped to her knees and snatched up the Keres sisters' dagger. She grabbed the reaper by the collar of his shirt and dragged him back a few steps. She crouched next to him and rested the dagger against Matthew's throat. "Back off, hound. Or your man gets it."

Nash growled and backed up until his bottom hit

the sisters. He clambered on top of the hags and laid out flat, pressing the hags into the ground.

"We never calculated in the stupidity of the hellhound," Lys grumbled.

"I'm more annoyed that we paid Hecate to spell the rope and it didn't work." Ana spat out a mouthful of hellhound fur. "He's shedding into my mouth," she wailed.

Lys banged her head on the ground. "Nothing goes to plan here.

"It's Point Muse. Trouble relocates here regularly." Lila turned to Marie. "What do you want?"

"What I've always wanted. Respect and *your* recipe."

"You get what you give. Respect isn't sabotaging my business," Lila growled.

Marie chuckled. "It wasn't hard, little mouse Janie was happy to help me in exchange for an employment package with Hestia."

"And when she refused?"

"Little girl grew a conscience." Marie snorted. "Apparently, you were too nice. She felt bad hurting your business. When the bodies started popping up, she got cold feet."

Lila shivered. All of this under her nose. Not much of a sleuth in the end. "You killed her."

"And the others." Marie giggled. "Everyone seemed so focused on the escaped death Daimons, I decided to take advantage of it."

"Told you so," Ana hollered from underneath Nash. "Not everything is as it seemed."

"One doesn't expect death spirits who live off violent death to tell the truth."

"That's your bias, Harrow. Not ours. We tried to help you," Lys sneered at Lila.

"The grave dirt and the warnings. If you didn't kill the victims, why the incisions on their hands?"

"Had to change our appearance so Shade wouldn't catch us before we could broker a deal. We sense death and just gathered the souls after that psycho killed them. But we didn't kill anyone ourselves."

"You were never after Geri or me at all?"

"Oh, we weren't happy with Geri turning traitor and we wanted our dagger back. But blood is blood. We wouldn't have killed her. Maybe given her a few bruises, though."

How could she have been so far off with her sleuthing? Lila tightened her hands into fists. "Why kill Geri, Marie? What did she do to you?"

"She overheard Janie and I discussing our plans for your bakery. She tried to blackmail me. That old woman wouldn't stand for anything to get in the way of her cupcake. I took her out. So easy." Marie smirked. "That gave me the idea to frame you for the murder. Meant I had leverage to negotiate for that brownie recipe. Win–win situation."

"Except all the other people you killed."

Marie shrugged. "Collateral damage. Worth the risk."

"Collateral damage?" Lila roared. Red heat flashed from her stomach to her throat and spewed out in heated words. "People died. Innocent people. You're evil and your company will never accept you back."

"They will when I give them your recipe. It's all about the bottom dollar at Hestia's. They only care about results, not how you achieved them. As long as you don't get caught." Marie pressed the dagger into the reaper's neck as he tried to fight her off in his still-drugged state.

"Mr. Grim was oh-so-helpful when he set up a meeting with me at the Inn. He even brought those vanilla cupcakes. Honestly, Lila. They were delicious and put such a spring in my step."

"Vanilla Viagra for the Soul cupcakes." Lila glared at Matthew. "They were for you, not to share with your kidnapper."

"Poor boy. He never realized I'd drugged the tea and conveniently became so clumsy. I just kept spilling my cup and the drug." Marie trilled a smug, gloating laugh. "So young and innocent."

"He's gonna be embarrassed when he sobers up."

"Which will be never since the dagger will slice and dice quite adequately."

"What do you want, Hestis?"

"Trade your recipe, your true recipe, and I'll let him go free."

Whatever it took, Lila wouldn't let another person die because of someone's obsession with sugar. "Fine. How do I write it down?"

Marie carefully dug out a pen and a crumpled piece of paper from her pocket. "Smart decision, Harrow."

Ignoring the sugar psycho, Lila carefully copied down all the ingredients. The only problem? *Her special ingredient.* The one that made her Decadent Death by Chocolate Brownies out of this world. A hefty dose of her Harrow magic. Once Marie learned that, either she'd take Lila or kill her. Either way, things wouldn't end so well for baker girl or the reaper. Lila finished the recipe and threw the pen at Marie. "Now what?"

"You slowly walk to me and hand over the recipe."

Best chance to take the villain down was to get her to lose control. One surefire way to do that...make her angry. Her heart in her throat, Lila advanced slowly on the killer. "The recipe won't help you, even if you follow it completely."

Marie bared her teeth. "You'd say anything right now."

"Probably. But it's the truth." Lila stood a small span away, the recipe held out. She stared down at Grim, and he slowly winked. Crafty reaper wasn't as drugged as he acted. Prepared for anything her reaper might try, Lila licked her lips. "The secret ingredient..."

Marie leaned forward and the dagger moved away from the reaper's neck a fraction. "Yes?"

"Is my magic. The only way the recipe becomes my Decadent Death by Chocolate Brownie is with Harrow magic."

"What? No," Marie wailed and reared back.

Grim took advantage of her distraction and surged up, struggling with Marie for the dagger.

Nash yelped and tumbled off the Keres sisters as they stood.

"Tally-ho," Elspeth cackled, and the cemetery lit

up like daylight as the wicked witch, Colin the Pug, and Matthew's father, Ed, charged in.

Ed Grim bolted into the melee, both reapers wrestling the now maddened Hestia descendant.

"Now, toots. Give 'em heck and Harrow." Colin belched and a tuna-scented cloud wafted over the area.

Hauling her arm back, Elspeth let go with a water balloon. It flew through the air, targeting Marie…and the two reapers. *Unfortunately*.

"Elspeth, no." Lila leaped to the side.

Marie saw the danger, and flung herself backward, but the reapers weren't so lucky. Ice encased their lower legs, chaining them effectively to one spot as the hex bomb encompassed the two reapers.

Lila rolled her eyes. "Harrow luck. The plan never turns out the way we want it to."

"Hey." Elspeth slammed hands onto her hips. "We're the rescue party. No dissing allowed."

"It doesn't matter. Nothing matters. I still have the recipe and the dagger. And coincidentally, those pesky reapers can't run away. Perfect ending to my plan." Marie advanced, dagger held out in front of her.

Lila's heart pounded in her ears. Father and son were sitting ducks. Ed's scythe lay on the ground out of reach. Lila felt in her pocket. She still had Matthew's. If she could just activate it. This was definitely a time where size mattered. She drew the reaper's weapon out of her pocket.

A grin split Matthew's face. "Never count a Harrow down."

Lila held the scythe out. "Come on, stick thing. We need to save your daddy and his father. Grow or something." The scythe quivered in Lila's hand and grew until it stood as tall as she did.

Marie screeched and lunged for the reapers.

Lila's scythe met the dagger, mid swing. Whooping, Lila pressed her advantage and pushed Marie back a few steps.

Unfortunately, Colin and Nash decided to help and galloped in. Entangled with paws and tails, Lila tripped and landed on the ground, scythe back to pencil size.

Chortling, Marie turned to Lila, dagger held over her head.

"You're not ruining our future deal, sister killer." Ana and her sister flew at Marie, hair streaming behind them, talons in attack position. Shadows formed around them until they were nothing but a cloud with fangs and talons.

Marie shrieked, dropped the knife, and scrambled back. The shadow cloud formed a barrier between Lila and Marie.

Elspeth cackled and clapped her hands just as lightning split the sky. "They're my kind of hag. Ever play poker, girls?"

Lila slumped on the ground. "That's just what we need. New poker buddies."

Nash stood over Lila, whimpering. She raised a hand and stroked his head. "It's all right. It all ended up okay. At least for us."

A sliver of slobber trailed from Nash's mouth and hit Lila's head with a plop.

"Mine" Nash's voice rumbled over Lila's head. Had her hellhound puppy just marked his territory?

Colin wiggled up next to Lila. "I think the young pup's a tad territorial. Me? I'm happy to spread my pugley love around."

Lila snorted. The image of Colin spreading love was not a happy one. In fact, the only thing that Colin spread around...

"Colin, don't you dare," Lila shrieked.

Colin smiled a wide toothy smile. "Elspeth prepped me for battle with tuna patties. They were delicious." He wiggled again, then sagged against Lila's side.

"*Noooo...*" Lila shrieked.

TWENTY

"It's mine. All mine." Marie Hestis, kidnapper and killer, shoved Lila's recipe into her mouth and chewed frantically. "Mine." She spewed small pieces of the paper out as she spoke. Shrieking, she dropped to the ground and tried to shove the paper and small lumps of dirt back into her mouth.

"Sorry about that. People tend to go a tad loco when they get near our shadow forms."

Lila smirked at the Keres sisters. "I think you looked great."

Elspeth slapped Lys on her back. "You need to show me how to do that shadow cloud. I'd like to send my enemies crazy. It'll add to my reputation."

Lila sighed and leaned against Matthew. "Like we need her any more wicked than she already is."

"Not our issue." Matthew tried to wiggle an ice-covered leg. "How long did she say the ice would take to melt?"

"Just long enough for me to hit my high score." Ed hollered in victory and went back to furiously hitting buttons on Elspeth's phone.

"Your mother will curse the Harrow name."

"Nah. She'll probably thank you for the peace. But I must admit, I never thought a Witch Invaders game on your grandmother's phone would keep him this quiet."

Lila snickered. "How do you think we keep Elspeth quiet when we need a few minutes of peace? Hand her the hipflask and her phone. It's the only sanity we have."

"My drama llama Lila, are you okay?"

"Great. There goes my peace."

Lila's father, Shade, and another man rushed into the cemetery, both skidding to a halt when they saw the babbling Marie and the now card-playing trio of Elspeth and the Keres Daimons.

Shade's blue eyes twinkled. "I see. Once again the Harrows had everything in hand."

Lila stood and walked to her father. "Actually, the Keres sisters had it in hand."

The other man stepped up, shorter than Shade,

with a receding hairline and bald patches amongst his stringy black hair. When he opened his mouth, a deep echoing voice vibrated, "Anaplekte and Achlys, step forward for your judgement."

"Now hold your underworld, Hades. Ana and Lys helped me. In fact, they haven't killed anyone in Point Muse. It was all that Hestia descendant."

"Be that as it may. Stygere is still dead. And my Daimons strayed from the path of their creation." Hades glowered at the poker playing hags.

On-the-fly, Lila came up with a plan. Hopefully, the death sisters wouldn't hate her, eat her heart, and send her soul to Hades.

Ana winked at Lila. "Do the deal, girl. We got your back."

Taking that as agreement, Lila plowed on. "The sisters did not kill anyone here. They only broke out of Tartarus because they wanted to see their sister and get the knife back. They wanted to get the hag band back together" Lila waggled her finger in Hades' face. "But you didn't answer any of their underworld emails. They've wanted to broker a deal for quite a while now. Some of this is your fault."

The God cleared his throat. "Persephone and I are on a break right now. I guess I haven't paid enough attention to my job."

"That's what you get when you hook up with a woman who doesn't eat sugar. It's just plain wrong." Lila shuddered at the horrible thought. "The girls want the old deal back, as long as they can remain as young as they are. They're happy to go back to working for you again."

Hades nodded. "But we have the problem of the third sister. Trio of Daimons, not a duo."

Lys pointed over her shoulder at a babbling Marie. "We'll take the crazy one. Train her up in Tartarus for a while, and then head out on work experience. Deal, H?"

Pursing his lips, Hades agreed. "A fitting punishment." He raised his voice. "Marie Hestis, you are judged and as punishment and reparation, you will serve as a Daimon under instruction from Anaplekte and Achlys. So says Hades." He stamped a foot on the ground which shook for a few seconds. "Right, gotta go. I'm betting that old crow, Hestia, has already sent a complaint through to my email." He rubbed his hands. "About time I had a fight with someone. Ciao, mortals."

"Don't you move, Hades."

The God of the underworld froze for a moment before visibly swallowing. "Amelia. Fancy seeing you here."

Lila's mother, Amelia Harrow, stomped up next to the God of the underworld. "My daughter risked her life for your runaway employees. You owe me," Amelia hissed at the God.

Hades backed away, hands up. "Whatever you want, you got."

Amelia beamed. "That's generous. I want Shade in Point Muse and we're renewing our vows. No more spending all his time in the Underworld."

"But..."

Amelia let loose the big guns. "Or maybe I should start spending my time in the underworld? Family can visit, can't they?" She winked at Elspeth.

"*No.* No need for that. I mean... You've got it. Shade can stay." Hades nodded his head, frantically. He clapped his hands and disappeared.

"Buttercup, I do." Shade grabbed his wife and bent her over his arm, peppering her face with sloppy kisses.

Lila slapped hands over her eyes. "I'm traumatized. Blinded. Have they finished yet?"

Matthew let out a roar of laughter. "Not any time soon by the looks of it."

"This is scarring."

Ed raised his head from Elspeth's phone. "A wedding is a blessing. Family is important. In fact,

Grim Incorporated has made a decision to settle a permanent office in Point Muse. Headed up by our youngest, Matthew." He winked at Lila. "Maybe there'll be another wedding in the family again soon?"

"Curse me now." Matthew hung his head.

"Gee, thanks for your vote of confidence." Lila sent the youngest Grim a pitying glance. "You have no clue the lengths matchmaking Harrows will go to."

Matthew paled.

"Feel my pain, reaper."

TWENTY-ONE

"I will never forgive her. My wrath is eternal."

"It's not that bad."

Lila glared at Matthew. "Are you on some kind of reaper drug you aren't sharing? I'm in a baby-pink marshmallow scratchy lace dress. At least you got to wear a suit."

"My powder-blue suit is as bad as your marshmallow dress and it's what your mother wanted. Now smile and throw your rose petals."

Lila pinned a smile on her face and took a handful of petals and pegged a bunch in Elspeth's cackling face, landing one right in her mouth.

Choking on the petal, Elspeth sent her granddaughter the evil eye as Lila and Matthew proceeded Amelia down the aisle.

"You'll pay for that," Elspeth hissed loud enough for everyone sitting around her to shift uncomfortably.

Matthew directed his gaze quickly away from Elspeth's fuming face.

"I'm a Harrow, I always pay for Elspeth." Lila concentrated on putting one foot in front of the other without falling on her face and the puffy marshmallow mess. Amelia had become bridezilla and threats had been made for those who didn't cooperate. Even poor Nash and Colin had been drafted into the wedding party. Both dogs padded away just in front of Lila and Matthew. They wore fluffy collars with trailing pink flowers.

Nash turned his head and woofed at Lila. Unfortunately, one of his trailing flowers tangled with Colin and both dogs sprawled on the ground in the middle of the aisle.

Lila tried to avoid the spread-eagled dogs, but with her fluffy meringue skirt, had no dodging capabilities. Her foot caught on Nash's pink flower collar and Lila flew.

Matthew shot out an arm and yanked Lila to the side but failed to account for a twitching Colin. Twisting to the side, he grunted as they both hit the aisle with Lila on top of him.

A pale pink curtain drifted over their heads, covering them from the audience's view.

Matthew settled Lila against him. "I have a strong sense of déjà vu happening right now."

"This was Elspeth. It has her wicked witch fingers all over it."

"So, we tripped. Can't be that bad."

Pointing to the pink cloud above them, Lila winced. "See that? That's my dress. Currently over our heads, like a parachute, exposing my nether regions in fluorescent pink girdle pants. It *is* that bad."

Lila lowered her head to the reaper's chest and wondered if the Grim family wanted an adopted daughter.

Because being Harrow was murder.

The End.

* * *

Want More?

You can sign up for my mailing list. It's for new

releases and no spam. Be the first to grab specials, new releases and freebies.

Sign up now.

https://www.kellyethan.com/newsletter

ABOUT THE AUTHOR

I want to thank everyone who spent the time to read my novel.

My world is small town magic, mystery and mayhem, with plenty of snarky laughs along the way.

With an overactive imagination and a love of all things that go bump in the night, it was natural to write cozy paranormal mysteries, but I also love paranormal romance. No matter the genre, I love sarcastic heroines who like to save the day and solve the puzzle.

With a busy and chaotic household, writing is my outlet for madness. I live in Australia and when not writing, I can be found plotting my next fictional murder or chasing after the family's ferocious hellhound.

Visit me today at my website or say hello on social media.

Website:
https://www.kellyethan.com

#8 The Nefarious Nemesis and the Wedding Jinx

Point Muse Cozy Paranormal Mystery Boxed Set: Books 1-3

Point Muse Cozy Paranormal Mystery Boxed Set: Books 4-6

Point Muse Cozy paranormal Mystery Boxed Set: Books 1-8

LILA HARROW: Point Muse Cozy Paranormal Mystery

Cookies, Curses and Christmas Corpses.

#1 Cupcakes, Corpses and Chaos

#2 Pies, Potions and Peril

#3 Sin, Sugar and Shadows

LILA HARROW Point Muse Boxed Set: Books 1-3

HOLLY HARROW: Point Muse Cozy Paranormal Mystery

Banshee, Vikings and Voodoo

#1 Banshee, Death and Disarray

#2 Banshee, Moonshine and Madness

#3 Banshee, Sea Monster and Sabotage

HOLLY HARROW Point Muse Boxed Set: Books 1-3

The Ghost Vein Mine Cozy Paranormal Mysteries

#1 Ghosts and Gold Dust

#2 Curses and Cold Cases

Non Fiction

Heart and Craft.

www.ingramcontent.com/pod-product-compliance
Lightning Source LLC
Chambersburg PA
CBHW051258210726
48287CB00002B/566